This book is a gift
from your librarian,

Miss DeMao.

(No Gateway School District or taxpayer money
was spent to purchase this book.)

Enjoy!

To Catch a Mermaid

To Catch A Mermaid

by Suzanne Selfors

Illustrated by Catia Chien

LITTLE, BROWN AND COMPANY

New York ⌁ Boston

For Walker

Little, Brown and Company

Hachette Book Group USA
237 Park Avenue, New York, NY 10017
Visit our Web site at www.lb-kids.com

First Edition: September 2007

ISBN-13: 978-0-316-01816-6
ISBN-10: 0-316-01816-3

10 9 8 7 6 5 4 3 2 1

Q-MT

Printed in the United States of America

Book design by Maria Mercado

Acknowledgments:

I feel very fortunate to have two excellent critique groups. Thanks to Carol Cassella, Dennis O'Reilly, Jonathan Evison, Anjali Banerjee, Sheila Rabe, Elsa Watson, and Susan Wiggs for reading the first draft. Thanks also to my hardworking agents, Kate McKean and Michael Bourret, and to my editor Jennifer Hunt and her assistant, T. S. Ferguson, and the staff at Little, Brown Books for Young Readers. Much appreciation to author Michael Collins, for always lending a sympathetic ear.

On the home front there's my mother, Marilyn, who deserves a big thank-you for being overwhelmingly supportive and downright fabulous. My father never got the chance to read this story, but I channeled his spirit when I created the character of Halvor. And I couldn't ask for a more enthusiastic audience than my children, Walker and Isabelle, and my niece, Maxine.

Finally, immeasurable gratitude to my husband, Bob, who could have said, "Are you nuts?" when I told him that, at age 39, I was going to start writing. But instead he said "Go for it." So I did.

Contents

"Sometimes a fish isn't exactly a fish"

—A very observant person with a magnifying glass

Chapter One:

FRIDAY the THIRTEENTH

Boom Broom awoke to find his little sister, Mertyle, look-ing for spots.

"It's a good day for spots," she announced, examining her knobby knees with a magnifying glass. While Boom rubbed sleep from his eyes and stumbled out of bed, his sister made up another ridiculous excuse for not going to school.

Last week she had suffered from orange tongue, thanks to an ancient Popsicle found at the bottom of the freezer. The week before, she had come down with ringing of the ears. "Could somebody answer that phone?" she had repeated whenever anyone walked into the room. Since the beginning of the school year, Mertyle had faked over sixty ailments including the common cold, yellow fever, weakness of the eyebrow, and nostril fungus. She had even claimed brain farts.

"Brain farts? That's just a saying for when you've done something stupid. No one's brain actually farts," Boom had pointed out.

"Well, mine just did," Mertyle had insisted, muffling her head with a pillow. "It's embarrassing and I don't want to go to school and have it happen in front of the entire fourth grade."

Boom knew the real reason Mertyle didn't want to go to school, and it had nothing to do with gaseous explosions of the brain. Mertyle didn't want to go to school because school lay beyond the front porch. The grocery store lay beyond the front porch, as did the public swimming pool and the ice cream shop, and she didn't want to go to any of those places either.

Mertyle had refused to step off the front porch for almost a year, ever since that terrible twister had touched down in the Brooms' front yard. The only person in the front yard at the time had been Mrs. Broom, tending her pink roses. The twister had sucked her away, like a vacuum cleaner grabbing a clump of cat fur. Boom and Mertyle had been at school, and when they'd come home, all that had remained of the twister was a big circle of dirt burned into the ground.

A tornado had never visited Fairweather Island before, though storms were common. The kind of storms that roll off the ocean, push over trees, and send waves and driftwood crashing onto the rocky beaches. From a bird's-eye view, Fairweather looked like two lumpy dollops of dough plopped down in the middle of nowhere. The larger dollop, where Fairweather's quaint harbor and colorful town lay, was attached to the smaller dollop by a narrow land bridge — too narrow for a road and too treacherous for a casual walk. Thus, the upper portion of the island remained wild and undeveloped.

That a twister had touched down just outside the Brooms' front door was difficult enough to understand. But the fact that Mrs. Broom, a very nice person indeed, could have simply vanished was beyond understanding, especially for Mertyle. The only thing found in the big circle of dirt was the magnifying glass that Mrs. Broom had always kept in her back pocket. The very next day, with her mother's magnifying glass in hand, Mertyle had refused to leave the house and had begun to fake being sick. She was determined not to miss the moment when her mother miraculously returned.

Mertyle wasn't the only Broom family member who refused to leave the house. After his wife's sudden disappearance, Mr. Broom stopped painting seascapes, which was how he had barely made a living. He announced that the twister would return, then he locked himself in his attic studio and asked for weather updates through the keyhole. Except for his dashes to the bathroom, or an occasional appearance in the kitchen to obtain something to eat, he had rarely been seen since. The world beyond the front porch had proven itself to be unpredictably dangerous, and Mr. Broom had decided to avoid it entirely.

In movies, twisters carry people to the Land of Oz and kill wicked witches. In real life, they inflict misery.

But Boom Broom wasn't like his little sister or his father. His mother's death didn't make him want to hide from the world. He wanted to kick the world — kick it good and hard and as often as possible.

A foghorn sounded in the distance. Ice crystals twinkled at the corners of the single-pane window. Boom shivered, tightening his bathrobe, and stared at the wall calendar that hung on his side of the room. One unfortunate outcome of living in the smallest house on Fairweather Island was that Boom and Mertyle had to share a bedroom — the only bedroom, in fact. Their tiny house consisted of a kitchen, living room, and closet on the first floor, a bedroom and bathroom on the second floor, and an attic on the third floor. Not much room for a family of three. And sharing a bedroom was the worst aspect. Why? Not because Mertyle snored or smelled bad in the morning, but because her side was aglow with coordinated pink curtains, pink pillows, and a pink comforter. She had painted a picture of a pink house surrounded by rainbow flowers and had tacked it to her wall. Her goldfish even swam around a pink castle. Boom, who had no interest in coordinating anything, especially anything *pink,* claimed his side of the room with piles of laundry, tousled blankets, and strewn books. But despite his attempts at camouflage, the first color he always saw when he awoke was pink, and that was no way to start a day.

He traced his finger across the calendar. Today was Friday, March thirteenth. He had circled the date in red — not because Friday the thirteenth was supposed to be unlucky but because it was the day Boom had been waiting for since the school year had begun. Today was the final game in the Kick the Ball Against the Wall Tournament. This would be Boom's last tournament because in three months he would graduate from sixth grade and move on to a new school. He was determined to leave Fairweather Elementary as a champion, glorified in lunchroom lore and playground stories as the best kicker ever. Boom smiled as excitement zapped his kicking foot.

"Yes, I'm definitely going to do spots today," Mertyle decided. She reached beneath her bed and pulled out the plastic bin that contained her tools of fraud. A black marker sat at the top of the bin, alongside a spritzer of water for mimicking sweat and a jar of fermented mayonnaise that smelled like vomit.

Marker in hand, Mertyle drew a few penny-sized spots

on the tops of her feet while Boom searched for his slippers. He kicked through a pile of dirty clothes. *Today is the day!* Mertyle added some spots to her arms. *Today, today, today.* Boom kicked his way across his side of the bedroom, sending Ping-Pong, soccer, and basketballs flying.

"Did you take my slippers?" he asked.

"Your slippers are under your geometry book," Mertyle said confidently. She added some spikes to a spot, turning it into a sunflower.

"Where's my geometry book?"

Mertyle, with a smug grin, pointed to behind the door. Sure enough, there lay the book with the slippers beneath.

"The only reason you know where everything is, is because I'm too busy to know where everything is," Boom told her. He spoke the truth. While he struggled with compound fractions and South American geography at school, Mertyle hung out in bed, eating Ry-Krisp and watching game shows. While he endured day after day of teasing because his shoes had holes, or because his pants were too short, Mertyle hid behind the walls of their small house, pretending to be sick, and examining things with their mother's magnifying glass. While he survived, Mertyle waited pathetically for a miracle to happen.

Boom couldn't stand the thought of staying inside all day. Sure, he felt sad too. Sadness had almost burnt a hole right through his stomach. He missed his mother as much as Mertyle did. Sure, he hated twisters too, but Boom had vowed that he would never pretend to be sick or shut himself away in the attic. He would never let the big dirt circle get the best of him!

Boom Broom had plans, and they involved the world beyond the front porch. Today, Friday, March thirteenth, was Boom's day.

Chapter Two:

A VIKING BREAKFAST

Breakfast!" Halvor yelled from downstairs.

Halvor served breakfast in the Broom household at 7:10 each morning. Boom bumped on his bottom down the steep staircase that led to the first floor — an uncomfortable yet efficient way to travel. The usual odors floated from the kitchen — Halvor's thick coffee that constantly percolated on the back burner of the potbelly stove, toasted rye bread, dark and crunchy and smothered in marmalade, and frying fish fillets. Never, ever, did Halvor make a normal breakfast. Boom longed for the cereal that was shaped like stars and drizzled with white frosting. Or the kind with tiny marshmallows that floated and turned the milk pale green. Halvor didn't cook bacon or eggs or pancakes or oatmeal, like the rest of the world. Every morning he made fish and rye toast and coffee.

"Sit down," Halvor barked as Boom entered. "Your fish is getting cold."

Halvor was the family cook, hired right after Mrs. Broom's disappearance. Mr. Broom had popped his head out of the attic to interview and hire Halvor. There wasn't enough money to pay a salary, so in exchange for cooking the children's meals, Halvor got a room in the garage, rent-free.

He was an old man, though Boom didn't know how old. About grandfather age. He had a big belly that sometimes didn't stay inside his shirt. He looked pregnant, but Boom knew that was impossible for males unless one were a sea horse. Halvor had a bald head, a bushy beard, hair growing out of his nose, and a slight Norwegian accent. "Where's Mertyle?" he asked.

"Here I am," Mertyle announced, glancing at the kitchen clock. "Sorry I'm late."

"You can bet that Erik the Red was never late for breakfast," Halvor said, adjusting his horned Viking helmet. He wore the helmet while cooking, to protect his scalp from flying grease. "Unless he was pillaging, for sure." Halvor mentioned Erik the Red at least ten times a day. He was a proud direct descendant of the dreaded Viking warrior and he belonged to a club called the Sons of the Vikings. They held meetings every Friday night.

"What's wrong with you this morning?" Halvor asked Mertyle as he slid a golden fillet onto her plate. Boom picked at his fish fillet, pushing the tiny white bones aside. He was so tired of picking through bones. Waffles don't have bones. Waffles don't have skin, either.

"I've got spots," Mertyle announced, lifting her pajama legs.

"Yah, I see. Spots. Okay, eat your fish."

Halvor was no dummy, but he never said to Mertyle, *I know you are faking these spots* or *I know you really don't have nostril fungus.* He just patted her on the head and let her stay home. Mr. Broom didn't seem to care either.

"Poor little Mertyle," he'd say through the attic keyhole. "You certainly can't go to school if you've got an ingrown toe hair. Stay inside, where it's safe. Stay away from the wind. That twister will be back, mark my words."

"Why don't you make her go to school?" Boom complained to Halvor that morning. He pulled two white feathers from his hair, escapees from his goose-down quilt. Boom rarely brushed his hair, and thus, bits of stuff could often be found in it. His hair grew straight up, like brown grass. "She's gonna flunk fourth grade."

"She's sick," Halvor replied, putting two more slices of bread into the toaster. "She doesn't feel well." No one ever asked Boom if *he* felt well. No one ever asked how things were going at school, or if he needed any help with that huge report on nest-building techniques of red-throated sparrows. His mother would have asked. She would have helped him when he had tried to build a sample nest out of sawdust and spit.

"Mertyle's nuts," Boom muttered.

Halvor dipped a piece of raw fish into some batter and tossed it into the frying pan. "Are you a doctor?" he asked Boom.

"Well, no," Boom replied, scraping chunks of marmalade off his toast. "But I can tell when someone's nuts." Boom had concluded that everyone in his family, except him, was nuts. He had even written a paper about it, but the teacher had given him a C minus with the comment, in red ink, that it wasn't nice to call other people crazy.

"You should keep your nose out of other people's business," Halvor advised, wiping his hands on his checkered apron. "If someone had told Erik the Red he was nuts, he would have hacked off that person's head, for sure."

Mertyle glared at Boom, angered by his disloyalty, but he believed he had only spoken the truth. It did absolutely no good to sit around the house and wait for someone to return who was never coming back. Besides, schoolwork had always been easy for Mertyle. She had never struggled with reading the way Boom had. She had the kind of brain that could get a scholarship for college, but no college would accept her if she flunked the fourth grade! Or if her brain turned to Jell-O from watching game shows all day long.

The coffee percolator whistled and gurgled as Halvor

sharpened his fish-gutting knife against a special stone. Boom ate his meal as best he could, deboning and scraping and picking until he managed to find a few edible morsels. He needed energy for the tournament. He had made it to the final round because he was the best kicker at Fairweather Elementary.

Mertyle examined some toast crumbs with the magnifying glass. She carried it everywhere. Before being sucked away, Mrs. Broom had worked as a fingerprint expert, so the glass was an extra powerful lens. "Each crumb is like its own world," Mertyle observed. "This one has a Grand Canyon, and this one has mountains." She saw things through that glass that no one else could see. "This crumb has an entire aqueduct system."

Yep. Completely crazy.

Boom loosened his bathrobe and wiped a bead of sweat from his forehead. While the rest of the house was ice-cold because there was no money for heat, the kitchen was balmy, thanks to the busy potbelly stove.

"You know, Halvor, on *Jeopardy!* last night . . ."

Boom groaned. Mertyle's know-it-all voice was more grating than most know-it-all voices.

". . . they had a category about Vikings."

"Oh?" Halvor smiled proudly.

"Vikings didn't actually wear horned helmets."

Halvor's face fell. "Of course they did." He adjusted his helmet. "Everyone knows that, for sure."

"No, they didn't," she insisted, moving her magnifying glass over a pile of fish bones. "It's a myth. And the *Jeopardy!* people should know because they have a whole building full of researchers."

Halvor folded his arms. He didn't like it when anyone questioned his Viking knowledge. In fact, it made his lower lip tremble. He pointed to the counter where two books on Viking lore lay. "I read. I know. Those game show people don't know because they aren't direct Viking descendants. How else would Erik the Red protect his head from hot fish grease?" Before Mertyle could make a counterpoint, Halvor stuck a finger in the air. "That reminds me, we are almost out of fish."

Could they be so lucky? Maybe that box of bow-tie pasta currently gathering dust in the pantry would find its way into a saucepan that night.

But Halvor pulled a ten-dollar bill out of the cookie jar and shoved it into Boom's hand. "After school, stop at the market and buy some fish."

That's right. Send the errand boy, as usual. Mertyle had two perfectly good spot-covered legs, but she never had to go to the market to buy fish, or go to the drugstore to buy Halvor's hemorrhoid cream.

"Why can't I get something else?" Boom asked. "How about hamburger?"

"Hamburger will make you constipated. Get fish. Fresh fish. Get it right off the boat if you can. I don't want fish

13

that's been sitting around on the dock. And I don't want anything too expensive, because we're running out of money. If your father doesn't start painting again, we're going to have to sell this house, for sure."

"We can't sell the house," Mertyle cried, dropping the magnifying glass onto her pile of crumbs. "How will Mother find us if we move?"

Silence fell over the kitchen. Even the coffee percolator stalled.

Halvor put his wide, speckled hand over Mertyle's spotted hand and gently squeezed. Poor Mertyle. When would she be able to face the truth?

The kitchen clock read 7:40. School started at eight. Boom asked to be excused, then ran upstairs to dress. He didn't want to be late for school. The last time he was late, Principal Prunewallop took away his lunch recess privileges, and that couldn't happen today because the tournament was scheduled for lunch recess.

Back downstairs, Boom put on his thin jacket. It provided little protection from the winter winds, but he owned nothing better. "Bring home Mertyle's homework so she'll get smart and her brain will stop farting," Halvor told him, handing over a sack lunch that smelled fishy, as it always did. Boom stuffed the lunch into his backpack, eager to be on his way. "Don't forget fresh fish," Halvor yelled after him.

"Okay, okay," Boom called back. But under his breath he made a wish that there would be no fish at the dock so he could bring home something else.

Chapter Three:

WINGER

Boom stepped off the sagging front porch and hurried across the big dirt circle. Fog hovered above the trees. The cold March air stung his nostrils. He kicked the walkway gate with his foot. It swung open, hanging from a single rusty hinge. He kicked it again. Then he stomped a dandelion seed ball with his secondhand sneaker. No one else had dandelion seed balls in their yard in March. Even though it was winter and most plants slept beneath the cold ground, dandelions grew between the cracks in the paved walkway that led from Boom's house to the street. In fact, dandelions suffocated the lawn, filled the forgotten window boxes, and had even taken root in the mailbox.

The yellow weeds had appeared right after the twister. Boom figured the seeds had been kidnapped by the swirling wind and deposited in their yard — come from some distant land where dandelions grew all year long. All the hacking and pulling in the world couldn't get rid of those stubborn transplants. It was bad enough having the smallest house on Fairweather Island, worse still to have one plagued by unsightly dandelions. Mertyle picked the ones that grew within arm's reach of the front door and put them in empty marmalade jars. Close inspection almost always revealed dandelion seeds in Boom's hair.

The only place the dandelions did not grow was in the big dirt circle.

Boom kicked the gate shut. It snapped free of the hinge and crashed onto the walkway. He shrugged his shoulders. It didn't really matter since the entire place was falling apart. Paint peeled off the house, gutters dangled dangerously, and duct tape held three windows in place. No longer did cherry red geraniums line the walkway, or bluejays chatter around overflowing bird feeders. No longer did polka-dot skirts or lacy underpants hang from the clothesline. When people passed by the periwinkle blue house at the end of Prosperity Street, they often stopped to gawk and shake their heads.

"That's the house where Mrs. Broom, a very nice person indeed, was sucked away by a tornado," they'd say.

"How terribly sad."

"Go away," Boom would yell from his bedroom window. He hated people staring. He wanted to kick people who stared.

Boom stepped onto the sidewalk and proceeded to kick things all the way up Prosperity Street — rocks, a Styrofoam coffee cup, even a growling dog who bit at his shoelaces. Kicking was the only thing Boom had going for him. He wasn't a genius, he wasn't graced with dashing good looks or a magnetic personality. But Boomerang Winslow Broom had been born with a better-than-average right kicking foot, slightly larger than his left foot and slightly thicker. A thing of beauty.

He paid no attention to the scenery on either side of the street, for it was the same old street he had walked along his entire life. And because he had never lived in a smog-filled city or a featureless development, he did not fully appreciate the picturesque quality of the stone houses that he passed, each painted in soft colors like sea-foam green, glazed apricot, and banana cream yellow — like candy chips on cupcakes. Most of the houses on Fairweather Island were made of stone because it stood up to the winter winds and the salty spray.

"Hey, Boom." His best friend, Winger, ran from his house and joined Boom on the sidewalk. Winger's full name was Victor Emmanuel Wingingham, so obviously he preferred Winger.

He handed Boom a Pop-Tart — blueberry with blue frosting. He always brought goodies for Boom because he had eaten at Boom's house many times since Halvor's arrival, so he knew what his friend was forced to consume. Boom shoved half the pastry into his mouth. He kicked an apple that must have fallen from someone's grocery bag, because all the apple trees were bare. He tried to savor the sweet blueberry filling — tried to let it linger on his tongue, but hunger overcame him. Who would have thought a simple rectangle of pastry and jam could taste so good?

"Are you ready?" Winger asked.

"Oh yeah, I'm ready," Boom proclaimed, spraying crumbs. The final game in the Kick the Ball Against the Wall Tournament was only a few hours away. Boom loved the game, but so did his archenemy, Hurley Mump. Hurley was last year's school champion, only because Boom had come down with chicken pox during the final week of games. Not fake Mertyle-drawn pox but the real thing that made his skin feel like flea food. But this would be Boom's championship year. So what if he didn't have professional kicking shoes like Hurley had, the kind those famous athletes wore? So what if he felt hungry most days, picking at a piece of smoked fish for lunch while Hurley chowed down on thick-cut turkey and cream-filled cupcakes? So what if everything in the universe seemed to always work against him? He had practiced all year and he had the best kicking foot in school. Today, 12:05, right after lunch. Boom vs. Hurley. Today was Boom's day!

"I bet seven dollars," Winger said. "You're gonna win for sure." Winger never played Kick the Ball Against the Wall. He wasn't allowed to because he wore glasses and had fake front teeth. But he kept score. He could keep score while opening ketchup packets and while picking all the shredded lettuce off a cafeteria hamburger. He could keep numbers in his head for days, without forgetting them. "No one can beat you."

"You got that right." They started up the sidewalk. Boom continued to kick the apple as they went.

"So, what's wrong with Mertyle this morning?" Winger always asked a lot of questions about Mertyle. Boom suspected that his best friend had a crush on his sister.

"She has spots," he told Winger. "She's nuts."

"What kind of spots? Like pimples? Pimples are disgusting."

"Sunflower spots," Boom said, but he didn't want to talk about Mertyle. He wanted to focus on the tournament. He needed to warm up his foot. He kicked the apple again, so hard that it flew over a picket fence.

Crash! The sound of breaking glass pierced the chilly air — a sound Boom had heard far too often.

"Hey!" a man shouted.

Boom and Winger didn't even look at each other. They took off at full speed, rounding the next corner like racehorses with blinders on. Boom's mind raced even faster than his legs. He couldn't get in trouble again. Not again.

Last week his soccer ball had dislodged a gutter, and yester-day his football had bonked the mail-lady on the head.

"Hey!"

Don't look back, he told himself. *Just keep running.*

But Winger wasn't fast enough, and when Boom did look back, Winger was in the clutches of Mr. Jorgenson, Fairweather's retired chief of police.

Chapter Four:

The PRINCIPAL'S OFFICE

Principal Prunewallop's office smelled like bad breath, which she had a constant case of. At Christmas time, all the teachers gave her boxes of peppermint candy, but Principal Prunewallop did not like peppermint. The next year they tried spearmint, but it turned out she was allergic to it. Then came wintermint and listermint, but she never ate them. Instead, she handed out the little green candies to her unlucky visitors.

Winger nervously unwrapped his listermint and popped it into his mouth. Boom stuffed his into his jacket pocket, where he had stuffed thirteen other mints from recent visits to the principal's office.

"Well, Mr. Broom and Mr. Wingingham. Your teacher tells me that you were both one hour late to class this morning." The principal's hair was pulled back so tightly that veins pounded at her temples. "Which one of you is going to tell me why you were late?"

Boom and Winger looked at each other without turning their heads. Winger bit down on his mint, then blurted, "Cat stuck in a tree."

Boom cringed. They had used that excuse last week. Winger never thought clearly when he got nervous. "My sister's sick again," Boom said. "She needed spot remover."

Principal Prunewallop drummed her long fingernails on her desk. "I am well aware of your sister's *condition*." She whispered the word "condition," and Boom felt his face go red. Seemed he wasn't the only one who thought that Mertyle was a lunatic. "In fact, I shall send the truant officer to your home next week to investigate." That would not be good.

The principal opened a rather thick file with Boom's name on the outside. Boom fidgeted and tapped his shoes together. His big toe stuck out a hole. Luckily, it was not his kicking foot. He shifted his bottom, which had gone numb. He hated this office, with its bad smell and uncomfortable chairs.

"This has been a difficult year for you, Mr. Broom," Principal Prunewallop stated, peering over the top of the file. She had pity in her voice, and Boom clenched his jaw. He wanted to kick people who pitied him. "Your rambunctious nature continues to interfere with your studies. And you, Mr. Wingingham, you should choose your friends more wisely."

It wasn't Boom's fault that Mr. Jorgenson, the retired chief of police, had lectured them for forty minutes. With his flabby chin and bulging eyes he had said, "Boys need discipline. That's what I always say. In my day, boys didn't run around in the street causing trouble. They had jobs from dawn until dusk. If they were bad seeds, then they were locked in cellars until they were eighteen, then shipped off to fight in wars. In my day, if a boy broke a window he went directly to jail." When exactly was "my day"? The middle ages? Mr. Jorgenson was nuts too.

Principal Prunewallop suddenly looked up from the file. "Did you hear that?" she asked. The only thing Boom had heard was Winger gagging on his mint. The principal turned to her office window, which overlooked the playground. She pressed her eye to a telescope that stood on a tripod. "Aha!" she exclaimed. "Just as I thought. I distinctly heard the sound of a bursting bubble." She stood and opened the window. Big orange underwear glowed through her stretchy white pants. She had the biggest butt Boom had ever seen.

With the principal's attention diverted, Winger spat out the horrid pieces of listermint into his hand. They glistened with saliva. Boom tipped back in his chair while Winger looked around for a place to dispose of the pieces. Boom knew they had to figure out a way to get out of this situation. Tardiness meant only one thing, and he couldn't miss lunch recess.

"Principal Prunewallop," Boom began, "the only thing I have to do after school today is buy some fish, and then I could come back and make up the time."

She ignored him. "Young lady in the green sweater," she called through a megaphone. "Yes, I'm speaking to you. Gum chewing is not allowed on the playground. Stop that right this minute. Don't you dare try to hide that gum beneath the monkey bars. You will report to my office immediately."

The principal whipped around so quickly that Winger dropped his mint pieces onto the rug, and Boom almost fell backward in his chair. "Now," she said, returning to her own chair, "back to the unfortunate business of your tardiness. That hour will be made up. You will both come to my office directly after lunch, today."

Today? After lunch? 12:05? She had to be kidding!

"But . . . ," Boom objected, with the intent of explaining that this was supposed to be his day. Boom's day.

She held up her hand to silence him. "I know all about the Kick the Ball Against the Wall Tournament, Mr. Broom. I am afraid that your irresponsible behavior has cost you a forfeiture. At twelve-oh-five, you and Mr. Wingingham will come to my office to work on your math skills. I look forward to instructing you."

"But —"

"No buts!"

Boom had no idea why principal was spelled with "pal." She instantly moved up his archenemy list to position number one. Forget her. He'd go to the tournament anyway. Even if it meant a hundred extra hours in her office, it would be worth it.

"And don't try to sneak out of this, Mr. Broom. I will be watching." She tapped a fingernail on the telescope.

Boom's special day broke into pieces, like a spit-covered mint.

On their way back to class, Boom and Winger passed the girl in the green sweater. She was taking very small steps toward Principal Prunewallop's office and sniffling. Boom clearly remembered his first walk toward that menacing door, where a sign read: AUTHORITY PREVAILS. "Don't worry," he said, trying to offer some comfort. "She doesn't spank." Which was the only nice thing he could say about the principal. The little girl managed a weak smile.

Winger started to sniffle too. "What are you crying for?" Boom asked irritably. "I'm the one who has to forfeit the game."

Winger took off his glasses and wiped his eyes. "I don't actually have the seven dollars I bet Hurley. He's gonna beat the daylights out of me."

Yes, Hurley *would* beat the daylights out of Winger. That was the kind of thing Hurley Mump would do. And he would call Winger names like "weenie," and "four-eyed freak." Boom knew the humiliation all too well.

He reached into his pocket and found the ten-dollar bill that was meant to buy the Brooms' evening meal. He handed Winger the money. "Just be sure to get me the change."

Once again, the universe had conspired against Boom Broom.

Chapter Five:

The REJECT SEAFOOD BUCKET

Boom kicked things all the way to the fish market.

Principal Prunewallop had made them divide decimals to obtain rounded quotients for the entire hour. Dividing decimals into rounded quotients was like eating cake for Winger, but Boom didn't even know what a stupid rounded quotient was. The principal had added an extra twenty minutes when she had caught him copying from Winger's page.

Hurley had told everyone that Boom had chickened out of the competition. Most of the students were too afraid of Hurley not to believe him. Hurley had proclaimed himself KBAW Champion of Fairweather Elementary. There wouldn't be another tournament for Boom, since he'd be at the middle school next year. It was his last chance to be school champion.

The only answer, Boom decided, was to schedule a rematch. He'd demand one, right after the flag salute at next Monday's assembly. He'd demand it in front of everyone, and Hurley would have to agree or he'd look like a chicken.

Boom adjusted his backpack straps. Mr. Foo had included two thick textbooks in Mertyle's huge pile of homework, and Boom had to carry the heavy load all the way to the fish market because Mertyle was a spoiled brat who stayed in bed all day and watched game shows. He kicked a huge rock that did not budge. "Ouch!" he cried. He kicked it again.

The wind picked up, but that wasn't unusual for Fairweather Island weather. A breeze could almost always be felt, no matter what time of year. Boom approached the quiet harbor. In summertime, the ferryboat would be depositing hordes of tourists, eager to fish the island's bountiful waters. The few inns that lined the shore would be blinking their NO VACANCY signs, and the pharmacy would be making a killer profit on seasick pills.

But it was March, and delivery vans and Fairweather residents were the ferry's only customers. Most of the fishing boats slept in their sheds. Only a few fishermen braved the winter sea, which could sparkle with sunshine one day and rumble with anger the next.

Boom walked past the empty stalls at the seafood market and down the dock to where a single boat was tied up. A couple of beefy men were unloading fish.

"Is that fresh fish?" Boom asked, remembering Halvor's instructions.

"Right out of the ocean," the man wearing a captain's hat replied. He scooped a fish from the boat's hold and tossed it to the other man, who then loaded it into a big cart.

"How much can I buy for three dollars?" Boom took out three one-dollar bills — all that remained after Winger had paid his bet.

"This be prime bluefin tuna," the captain told him. "You can't buy one of these for less than ten dollars."

Just as Boom had expected. That darn universe again. Halvor would be steaming mad. Viking descendants have notoriously short tempers.

"But I need some fresh fish," Boom explained, repositioning the backpack. "All I got is three dollars."

The captain stopped scooping for a moment. He took off his hat and wiped his sweaty forehead with his upper arm. "Well, lad, you can have whatever you want from that bucket." He pointed to the end of the dock. "That there be the reject seafood that found its way into me net. Watch your fingers. There's some nasty critters in there."

Reject seafood? That didn't sound very tasty. A cold wind stung Boom's face as he walked down the dock to where a white bucket rocked back and forth. Some clicking crabs clung to the bucket's edge. A few had already escaped and were scuttling across the planks. Boom peered into the bucket. Green sea grass floated at the surface, and something moved beneath. The bucket rocked again, and a shiny blue-green tail emerged. It flapped about, then disappeared beneath the grass. It looked like a thick, meaty tail that Halvor could chop to his heart's content. He wouldn't have to know it came from the reject bucket.

Something that's still alive is about as fresh as it gets.

Boom pushed up his jacket sleeve and stuck a hand into the cold water. The tail felt slimy and it slipped from his grip. Water splashed onto Boom's face.

Stupid fish.

He took off his backpack and tried again, this time with both hands. The fish struggled as Boom grasped the tail's tip. The fish's body was so big it was wedged tight. With a deep breath, Boom pulled with all his might and the fish came free. Tangled in a mess of sea grass, it fought desperately, but Boom managed to shove it into his backpack, right on top of Mertyle's homework.

Her own fault, he thought, as he closed the zipper.

The backpack started flip-flopping down the dock. "Hey!" Boom called, chasing after it. He managed to reach it just before it fell off the edge. He picked up the pack and slipped his wet arms through the straps. Now the pack was uncomfortably heavy. He shook a crab off his shoe, then walked back to the boat.

"Here's my three dollars," Boom said, holding out the bills.

"That be quite a fish," the captain said with amusement as the backpack lunged side to side. "You sure you want it?"

"*I'm* not the one who wants it," Boom grumbled. "I'm sick of fish." He kicked a clamshell. It soared over the boat and landed in the water.

The captain folded his arms and stared at Boom, long and hard. "I can tell when a man's had a bad day," he said. "You keep your money, lad. You be needing it for antacid if you eat that fish."

Boom put the money back into his jacket pocket. "Thanks," he said. "Hey, what kind of fish is it anyway?"

"Beats me," the captain replied. "I've never seen the likes of it in all me years of fishing. Fought like the devil to get free. I give you fair warning, lad — a fish like that comes from the darkest part of the ocean, where we men aren't meant to go. You be either brave or stupid to try to eat a fish like that."

Chapter Six:

FISH for DINNER

"Yuck!" Mertyle exclaimed, when Boom dumped the contents of the backpack onto the kitchen table. She picked up one of the textbooks. Fish juice dripped from its pages. "Great," she said sarcastically. She picked up a soggy division sheet. A few pieces of seaweed clung to the homework's edge. "And how am I supposed to write on this?"

"With a pencil and you're welcome," Boom snapped. It might have been nice to come home to just a little bit of sympathy. But neither Halvor nor Mertyle understood the importance of KBAW tournaments. Mr. Broom, on the other hand, was a huge fan of kicking. Or used to be, before he locked himself away. More than anything, Boom wanted to run up the two flights of stairs and tell his father about Principal Prunewallop's unjust ruling. His father would call the school and demand that rematch. His father would stand up for him. His father would . . .

Boom sighed. His father had enough to worry about. Boom would have to fight his own battles.

"My goodness," Halvor said, looking at the madly flapping pile of green sea grass. The tail reached out and overturned the salt and pepper shakers and a jar of dandelions. "What kind of fish is it?"

Boom shrugged. "He didn't say."

"Just keep that fish from bouncing off the table while I sharpen my knife," Halvor ordered, opening a drawer. Fluffy, Halvor's cat, jumped up onto the table and hissed as the fish flopped close to the edge. Mertyle pushed the soggy textbook aside.

"What a strange tail," she said, cleaning her magnifying glass with a napkin. "Such bright colors. This looks like a tropical fish."

What was she talking about? Tropical fish didn't live in the cold ocean that surrounded Fairweather Island. Boom shook his backpack over the sink, clearing out sand and kelp.

The fish kept moving about. Mertyle grabbed a wire basket from the counter, dumped out the dried heels of rye bread that Halvor saved for the squirrels, then set the basket over the fish, trapping it. She took up the magnifying glass and peered through the wires. "Wow. You've got to see these scales," she said. "Each one is a perfect triangle. Some of them have weird markings."

"Out of the way," Halvor barked, fish-killing knife in hand. He plucked off the basket. The fish began to flop again, upsetting the cat and a jar of sugar. "Watch out," Halvor warned as his big knife swooshed through the air, missing the fish by a mere inch. "That's a quick fish," he complained, trying to free the blade from the table's surface. "I've never seen such a fish. I need a special Viking artifact from the garage."

As Halvor went out the kitchen's side door, the fish slipped off the table's edge. Boom caught it in midair. Just as he placed it back on the table, it bit him.

"Ouch," he cried, holding up a bleeding pinkie. "It's a shark."

The fish growled.

Mertyle and Boom jumped back. The cat, truly freaked out, retreated to the corner with its back arched and its hair sticking straight up like Boom's.

"I didn't know sharks could growl," Boom said.

"They can't." Mertyle slowly approached the table. "They had an entire *Jeopardy!* category on sharks last week. Sharks can't growl and they don't have scales, either. Something's fishy here. I need another look. Hold it still with the basket."

Boom didn't want to get bit again, so he put on a pair of Halvor's oven mitts. Then he ran around the table trying to catch the mass of writhing seaweed. After some effort, he slammed the wire basket over their evening meal. Mertyle climbed onto the table and picked up the magnifying glass again. "I can see the teeth. Wow! They're supersharp, two full rows of them. But that seaweed is in the way. I can't see anything else."

The fish started to chomp on the metal basket until it made a big hole. Boom poked the end of the sugar spoon through the hole and tried to push aside the strands of sea grass. "Nice fishy, fishy," he cooed. A softer growl sounded as Boom untangled the grass. "Nice fishy, fishy." The strands parted.

Both Boom and Mertyle gasped with the force of a vacuum cleaner hose. Beneath the hole in the basket peered a little green face. It turned a pair of violet watery eyes up at them and blinked long black lashes. Out reached two little arms. Human arms with little human hands.

Boom thought his heart would stop beating.

The garage door slammed. Boom and Mertyle ran to the kitchen window. Halvor carried an enormous axe over his shoulder as he approached. "Oh no," Boom said, recalling the stories that Halvor often told them. "That's the axe that Erik the Red used to fell trees in a single swoop."

"No," Mertyle corrected. "That's the axe Erik the Red used to cut off the head of the fire-breathing sea monster."

Cut off the head?

Boom and Mertyle looked at each other and, without speaking, knew exactly what needed to be done.

Chapter Seven:

The THING on the BED

Boom dumped the thrashing creature onto Mertyle's bed, then ran back downstairs to deal with Halvor. The cat bounded past, almost tripping Boom on the stairs.

A coat of green slime covered the kitchen table. "Where's the fish?" Halvor asked, holding the axe over his shoulder.

Think fast, think fast. "Cat took it."

"What do you mean the cat took it?" Halvor asked.

"Mertyle and I turned our backs, just for an instant, and Fluffy dragged it off." Boom thought he sounded very convincing. He kept his voice steady, which was really hard to do, considering he had just seen a fish with arms.

"How can a little kitty drag off such a big fish?" Halvor challenged.

Good point. *Come on, come on, think of something.*

"The domestic cat is a direct descendant of the lion," Boom stated. If there was one thing Halvor understood above anything else, it was the importance of being a direct descendant. "Never underestimate the power of direct descendancy."

Halvor stroked his beard as he mulled it over. "Yah, come to think of it, she does like to torture cockroaches. Which way did she go?"

Boom pointed to the cat door that provided access to the side yard. Fluffy used the side yard as a litter box. Halvor stomped out of the kitchen, calling, "Here, Fluffy, Fluffy, Fluffy."

Boom ran back upstairs. As he rushed into the bedroom, Fluffy leapt onto Mertyle's dresser, her eyes glued to the thing that flipped and flopped on the carnation pink comforter. The thing started growling again, not like a frightened dog or an angry bear, but the kind of gurgling growl, Boom guessed, that might come from a frightened dog or angry bear if it swam underwater.

Boom locked the bedroom door. His heart beat so fast he feared it might burst through his jacket.

The blue-green tail arched, then smashed Mertyle's box of Ry-Krisp that she snacked on while watching game shows. It arched again and thwacked the wall, leaving a trail of green slime.

What was that thing?

"Here, Fluffy, Fluffy, Fluffy," Halvor called from the side yard. "Let the big fishy go. Give the big fishy back to Halvor."

A green hand reached out and felt along the bedding until it found a piece of a Ry-Krisp. The cracker disappeared into the mass of sea grass, and an unmistakable chomping sound filled the room, followed by a little underwater burp.

It was hungry.

The cat sat frozen on the dresser, like a stuffed animal. Boom felt frozen too, like his feet were made of cement. But Mertyle, who was afraid of facing reality, courageously approached the bed.

Mertyle handed the wiggling fingers another cracker, and sure enough, the little hand greedily accepted it. Crumbs flew, accompanied by more chomping, then another burp. After three more crackers, the tail stretched out and the creature quieted. A full two minutes passed before Boom edged forward. The thing seemed to have fallen asleep. Its breathing came slow and raspy, like waves rolling onto shore. The sound made Boom feel sleepy as well.

Mertyle clutched the magnifying glass and gave the creature a closer look. "Each strand of sea grass springs from its head," she whispered. She took a hair ribbon from her desk and carefully gathered the grass, strand by slimy strand, into a high ponytail, exposing the wide face. Its eyes were closed and it had stuck a thumb into its mouth. The face was human, mostly, except for the extra-flat nose. And the fact that it was green and had sea grass for hair. And killer teeth.

Neither Boom nor Mertyle said anything for a long time. Words seemed so insignificant. Words could not begin to describe the amazement that flooded Boom's veins. If ordered to write an essay, at that very moment, about how he was feeling, Boom simply would have written the word "wow" over and over and over. Could he really be seeing what he thought he was seeing?

He scratched his head, setting a couple of dandelion seeds free. "I can't believe it," he murmured. "It can't be." Fluffy leapt onto the headboard to get a closer look.

"It is," Mertyle said with confidence. "The tail is made of scales while the upper half is covered in skin. It has nipples, a belly button, and ten fingers. It's a baby mermaid."

"I just can't believe it." He really couldn't. This wasn't possible. Yet the impossible slept on Mertyle's bed.

Mertyle peered through the magnifying glass at the tail. "Come to think of it, I'm not sure if it's a mermaid or a merboy."

"Huh?" Boom looked at the tail. Obviously he knew how to tell the difference between a boy person and a girl person, but he didn't know how to tell a boy fish from a girl fish. It just looked like a tail.

"Let's just call it a baby for now," Mertyle decided. "A merbaby."

A merbaby? Boom Broom didn't walk around in a fantasy world, like the rest of his family, believing that a dead parent could return or that it's possible to avoid danger by staying inside. No, Boom Broom had his feet, both the big one and the regular one, planted firmly on the ground. There had to be a better explanation. "Maybe it's some kind of mutant from nuclear waste that got dumped in the ocean or some toxic chemicals that leaked from a barge. Two-headed fish pop up all the time. I've seen photos of them in the *International Inquirer* newspaper. This is probably just a freak of nature."

"It's a merbaby."

"See if it's got a zipper," Boom said. "In case it's a costume." Someone might be playing a trick on them. Maybe this was one of those hidden-camera shows.

Mertyle lifted the tail, continuing her inspection. A little squirt of yellow landed on the comforter.

"It's a real tail," she said, plugging her nose. "And that's real merbaby poop."

The baby scrunched up its face and squirted out another little blob. "Disgusting," Boom groaned. The stuff smelled like Halvor's hot fish nectar. Boom opened the window to get rid of the stench. A blast of winter air quickly deodorized the room.

The bedroom window looked out onto Prosperity Street and the Mumps' house across the way. The Mumps' minivan pulled into their driveway. Daisy Mump, Hurley's little sister, leapt out, as did three other girls. They carried sleeping bags and overnight cases and giggled when they pointed at the Brooms' house, a run-down shack compared to the Mumps' stone mansion. But before the girls caught sight of Boom at the window, Halvor stormed into the front yard, still holding Erik the Red's axe. The polished silver blade reflected the cloudy sky.

"You girls seen a big fish flopping about?" he hollered over the broken picket fence. The girls screamed and ran into the Mumps' house.

"Put that thing away!" Mrs. Mump scolded, pointing at the axe. Her coat stretched across her chest like she had torpedoes under it. "You're going to hurt someone."

"I'll do as I please in my own yard," Halvor cried, shaking the axe.

"Well, that's not really *your* yard," Mrs. Mump yelled, grabbing her purse. "You're just a servant and you aren't doing your job because that yard is an eyesore. It's the ugliest yard on Fairweather Island. Look at all those horrid weeds. Why don't you do something about them?"

"Mind your own business!" Halvor hollered. "For sure!"

Mrs. Mump stomped her high heel. "How dare you speak to me like that. If I see you swinging an axe anywhere near my daughter again, I'll call the police." She stormed into her house, slamming the door.

Feeling the sting of Mrs. Mump's rude words, Boom closed the window. The commotion had awoken the baby. It opened its fang-filled mouth and began to whine — a sound like wind seeping through a crack under the door. Boom stepped toward it and the whine turned into a growl. He took another step — another growl. But it didn't growl when Mertyle sat down on the bed and scooped it up. It peered at her with its watery eyes and made a little bubble.

"Why does it growl at *me*?" Boom asked. "I'm the one who saved it from the reject seafood bucket." He stepped forward again and the baby whipped its head around and gnashed its teeth at him.

Mertyle smiled. She actually smiled. To Boom's knowledge, Mertyle hadn't smiled since the twister. "I'm going to keep it," she said with a giggle. "It's the cutest baby I've ever seen."

Cute? It smelled like mud and left green slime on the walls and yellow puddles on the bed.

"But we can't tell Halvor," she added. Boom knew exactly what she meant.

Halvor hated merfolk. During the past year, as he had worked as their cook, he had shared many stories with the Broom children — stories of Viking raids and great battles, of Viking journeys across the unknown sea, and of encounters with strange creatures. To the Vikings, the most feared sea creatures were the merfolk, who stirred up gales and lured sailors to their deaths with an eerie song.

"On a night as black as coal," Halvor had told them, "a pair of green hands pulled Erik the Red's beautiful wife, Matilda, overboard and drowned her. All that remained was a shred of her dress hanging on the rail and a conch shell, the mark of the merfolk. Sick with grief, Erik the Red declared that merfolk would be Viking enemies until the end of time and that all Vikings, and their direct descendants, were obligated to kill them on sight."

Boom swallowed hard, imagining the axe slicing through green baby flesh. Even though it had bit him, it didn't deserve to have its head chopped off. "You're right. We can't tell Halvor."

"We can't tell *anyone* about it," Mertyle said, her eyes widening.

"Why not?"

"Because the scientists will come and poke the baby with equipment, just like in *E.T.,* and the government will try to put it in a cage, just like in *King Kong.* Then the circus will stick it into a tank and people will point fingers at it." She tightened her arms around the baby. It began to chew on a strand of Mertyle's hair.

Boom sat down on his bed to think this out. How could they possibly hide this thing from Halvor and the rest of the world? If this creature was truly a merbaby, wouldn't that be the most amazing discovery of the twenty-first century? Having discovered it, wouldn't he become the most famous kid in the entire world? And wouldn't that make Hurley crazy with envy? Sure, being Kick the Ball Against the Wall champion was a big deal, but discovering a creature that no one believed actually existed was as big as stepping on the moon. Bigger!

But Mertyle wanted to keep it a secret and hide it in their room like a stolen toy. What would happen when it grew up? Like when Winger had talked his mom into buying a baby boa constrictor and then the snake had tripled in size and swallowed their cat! Exactly how big do mer-teeth get?

"I'm not sure it's such a good idea," Boom said. "We don't know how to take care of a merbaby."

"Please, Boom. I'll take care of it. I know you found it, but it doesn't really like you. You don't have to do anything. It can stay here with me and watch game shows." She stroked its hair. "I think it's an orphan. It needs me."

Boom looked over at the wall calendar, where the big red circle marked today as his day. This wasn't at all what he had expected.

Mertyle hugged the creature, and the gloom that she had worn for the past year fell away like a heavy cape.

"Sure, Mertyle," he said with a sigh. "You can keep it."

Chapter Eight:

The GOLDFISH SACRIFICE

With no fish for dinner, Halvor served toast and marmalade, which Boom and Mertyle ate as fast as they could. He left for his Sons of the Vikings meeting at seven. Once he had disappeared down the dark street, Mertyle grabbed a book from the living room coffee table and rushed back upstairs. "It's one of Halvor's Viking books," she told Boom as he followed. Boom knew the book well — a poorly bound manuscript with shaggy edges and well-worn pages. "The facts might be questionable but it's the only one that has a section on mermaids." Mertyle began to read while the baby took another nap.

"It says here that mermaids have no tongues," she told Boom as her fingers flew across the page. "They can't talk. They only sing. It says that mermen sometimes eat their young. Oh, that must be why the baby doesn't like you."

"Eat their young? Let me see that." Boom reached for the book, knocking a lamp over in the process.

The baby woke up and began to cry, but it was no ordinary cry. The cry filled the room like a whistle, darting between the sheets, boomeranging off the corners, and shooting down the tunnels that led to Boom's eardrums. When it had possessed every possible space in the bedroom, the cry overflowed into the rest of the house.

"Hello?" Mr. Broom called from the attic.

"Oh no," Boom moaned. He ran up the narrow stairway that led to the third floor.

"What's that odd noise?" Mr. Broom asked. Boom could see only one side of his father's face through the crack in the attic door. Mr. Broom had grown a long beard, and the eye that peered out was wild with panic. "Such a strange noise. It sounds like a dangerous sort of wind."

"It's . . . it's just a new teakettle," Boom lied.

"Not the wind?"

"Not the wind."

"Not another twister?"

"Not another twister."

Mr. Broom nodded, then shut the door. Boom ran back down the stairs.

"I think it's hungry," Mertyle hollered above the earsplitting shriek. She shook the Ry-Krisp box, but only crumbs fell out.

Boom stuck his fingers into his ears, but that didn't help. The sound managed to seep through his cells. It was the most annoying sound in the world. Worse than a car alarm. Worse than Principal Prunewallop droning through her megaphone. Even worse than Mertyle's know-it-all voice. If an earwig had crawled into Boom's ear and sung "Ninety-nine Bottles of Beer on the Wall," it would have been less annoying than the merbaby's cry.

Mertyle hurriedly turned the page in Halvor's book. Then she shrugged and shook her head. "Doesn't say anything about what merbabies eat."

"Babies drink milk," Boom yelled.

The shrieking continued as they rushed downstairs. The sound oozed its way through the single-pane windows of the tiny house. While Mertyle held the baby, trying to calm it, Boom poured milk into a plastic water bottle. Then he squirted the milk into the creature's tongueless mouth. The baby quieted, but only long enough to spit the milk onto Boom's face.

"Hey," Boom complained, pointing his finger. "Bad baby."

"Did you warm it?" Mertyle asked. "Babies like warm milk." She had wrapped the creature in one of her doll blankets. The seaweed ponytail stuck straight up. The mer-baby looked like a troll. An angry troll.

Boom put a saucepan on the stove and began to heat the milk. He knew how to do this because Mrs. Broom had taught him how to make hot chocolate. He wiped milk from his eyebrows and wondered if merparents spanked their children.

"Shhh," Mertyle urged as Boom stirred. The baby cried even louder. One of the dandelion jars shattered from the sound wave's impact. "The milk is almost ready." But Boom had turned the burner on too high, and the scent of scorched milk rose from the stove. "Oh, that's just great," Mertyle complained.

"If you're so smart, then why don't you do it?" he asked defensively. He turned off the burner, grabbed Halvor's oven mitts, and dumped the pan into the sink. The last of the milk lay curdled on the bottom, charcoal black. The baby started to shriek again, and a full marmalade jar exploded on the pantry shelf.

"Do we have any more rye bread?" Mertyle cried.

There was no bread in the pantry, and Halvor had already fed the leftover heels to the squirrels. Boom scraped a spoonful of marmalade off the shelf, careful to make certain it contained no bits of glass. He poked the spoon into the baby's open mouth. Like the milk, the marmalade shot out between the sharp teeth. This time Boom ducked. The orange blob landed with a splat on the wall. But the creature didn't start shrieking again. Instead, it pointed at the kitchen window, where Hurley Mump was pressing his face.

Mertyle gasped and turned her back to the window. Someone started pounding on the kitchen door. Mertyle pulled the edges of the doll blanket around the baby and ran upstairs. "Go away," Boom yelled at Hurley, who scowled menacingly. Someone pounded at the kitchen door again.

"What's going on over here?" Mr. Mump asked when Boom opened the door. He kept his blond hair shaved close to his scalp, just like Hurley did. "What's that terrible noise that's been coming from your house?"

Hurley appeared at his father's side, his eyes narrowed. He smirked in the way he always smirked at Boom. An *I'm so much richer than you are* smirk. An *I'm the KBAW champion* smirk.

But had he seen the baby?

"Teakettle," Boom said. "We got a new teakettle."

"Teakettle, you say?" Mr. Mump weighed about three hundred pounds. Barbecue sauce glistened around his lips. "That teakettle disturbed our dinner. I suggest you get rid of it or I shall call the police."

"Yes, sir," Boom said, faking a smile as he shut the door. Mr. Mump always acted like he owned the neighborhood.

From the bedroom window, Boom and Mertyle watched Mr. Mump and Hurley cross the street. "I think Hurley saw," Boom said. The baby's shriek had weakened to a low moan. Mertyle looked at it worriedly.

"We've got to feed it something," she fretted. "If it won't eat marmalade, what can we give it?"

"I don't know." Boom was still picturing Hurley's smirk. "You told me that you'd take care of it." Trying to hide a merbaby was possibly the worst decision he had ever made, worse even than trying to outrun Mr. Jorgenson. For a fat guy, that man could move surprisingly fast.

"Please, Boom. It's got to eat or it will die."

Suddenly, the baby stopped moaning and reached out both hands toward Mertyle's desk, where, along with a can of pencils and a stapler, sat the goldfish bowl. "Oh, of course," Boom realized. The creature came from the ocean so it would eat food from the ocean. "Why didn't I think of that before? It wants fish food." He picked up the cylinder of SuperGrow Fish Food from beside the goldfish bowl and sprinkled some into his hand, offering the flakes to the baby. But the baby ignored the flakes and continued to reach out. "Fish food," Boom explained, offering the flakes again. The baby shook its head and started that mind-numbing, bowel-loosening shriek. If the shriek disturbed Mr. Mump's barbe-cue feast again, they'd be in big trouble. Mr. Mump would call the police, and the police would come and want to speak with Mr. Broom. They'd discover the merbaby for sure. They might also discover that Mr. Broom had been ignoring his children, and they'd take Mertyle and Boom away to a fos-ter home, and they'd put Mr. Broom in a mental institution. And what if they discovered Halvor's Viking weapons collec-tion in the garage? Those things had to be illegal.

Boom took a long look at the fishbowl. Ted the Goldfish swam around the pink castle the way he always did. Boom reached his hand into the bowl. He had to make the shriek-ing stop.

"Not Ted!" Mertyle cried.

Boom pinched Ted's tail between his thumb and middle finger and flung the surprised goldfish through the air, right into the baby's eager, open mouth. The ferocious teeth snapped shut and the blue-green tail wiggled with delight. The shrieking stopped. Boom felt slightly nauseated by what he'd done.

"Ted?" Mertyle whimpered.

The baby burped and immediately fell asleep. Mertyle stared at the empty fishbowl, where Ted had been swimming circles for two years. Colored pebbles floated around, stirred-up from Boom's hand. "Poor Ted." She sighed and laid the baby on the comforter. Its little green chest rose and fell with every raspy breath.

"I didn't know what else to do," Boom explained, feeling really bad, regardless of necessity.

Mertyle nodded. "He gave his life for a good cause. I'm going to make a tombstone for him and write that on it." She picked up her magnifying glass and began to inspect the merbaby's tail again. "There are really strange markings on some of the scales. They kind of look like little drawings. What do you think?"

Boom looked through the lens, but he didn't see any drawings. Mertyle always saw strange things with that lens. "I don't know what to think anymore." He tried to shake the image of Ted being sliced by those teeth.

Boom pulled back his covers and climbed into bed with his clothes on. He needed the extra layers since the room was so cold. When would they have enough money to turn on the heat? If March turned any colder, he might have to start sleeping in the kitchen.

All of the day's disappointments and all of the day's excitements had exhausted him. Mertyle turned off the light and lay down next to what was supposed to have been their evening meal. "I'm so glad you found it," she whispered. "I always thought they weren't real."

Boom nodded, too tired to speak. Usually when he drifted off to sleep, he secretly listened for the sound of his mother's heels coming up the walkway. But tonight, as he closed his eyes, he drifted along with the baby's sea-soaked breaths.

Chapter Nine:

ERIK the RED

The odor of percolating coffee crept up the stairs and seeped under Mertyle and Boom's bedroom door. Even though it was Saturday morning, Halvor still served breakfast at 7:10. Boom rolled out of bed, bleary-eyed. "So tired," he mumbled. Something had kept him up half the night, but his blurry brain couldn't remember what.

"I don't think I should go to breakfast," Mertyle said as Boom pulled on a pair of socks that Fluffy the cat had slept on. "I can't leave the baby."

"The baby?" Boom's brain kicked into gear. Hadn't all that simply been a dream? After all, the Cheshire Cat turned out to be a dream and the Cowardly Lion did too. Boom rubbed his eyes and stared at the green creature that was sleeping amidst waves of pink comforter. It hadn't been a dream. Amazement flooded Boom once again, from the tips of his fingers to the tips of his toes.

"Tell Halvor I'm sick. Tell him I've got ringworm," Mertyle said.

"You're never sick on the weekend," Boom pointed out. "Halvor will get suspicious if you don't go downstairs. He might come up here."

"If I leave it alone, it might start shrieking again."

That would be a problem, to say the least. Boom couldn't use the teakettle excuse because Halvor knew that there was no teakettle — coffee only in the Broom household. "As soon as it wakes up, it's going to be hungry," Mertyle warned. "Ted wasn't very big. What are we going to feed it today?"

"I don't know," Boom said. "I have three dollars but I don't think that will buy much. Do you have any money?"

"No."

"I guess I could go back down to the dock and see if there's still some stuff in the reject seafood bucket. Maybe the baby would eat some of those crabs."

"Good idea. In the meantime, I'll try to sneak some of my breakfast upstairs."

Mertyle wedged the sleeping baby between pillows so it wouldn't fall off the bed. Boom figured there was no need to change out of the jeans and sweatshirt he had slept in. It wasn't like any of his other clothes were cleaner, piled as they were in the corner of his room. The walk to the harbor would take him right past Winger's house. Boom had agreed not to tell anyone about the merbaby, but Winger wasn't just *anyone*. Boom couldn't keep the discovery of the twenty-first century from his best friend.

Halvor was at work in the balmy kitchen, humming happily. His armpits were damp with sweat. "I bought some cod fillets at the all-night Thrifty Mart, half-price, and some day-old bread," he told the kids when they sat down in the painted chairs. He stood over the black frying pan, his Viking helmet askew. The cat wound between his thick legs, begging for bits of fish skin. "You are a very bad kitty," Halvor scolded. "Bad kitty for stealing my big fish last night."

A jar of tartar sauce sat on the table, alongside a pile of buttered rye toast. Boom grabbed two pieces, then headed for the door. "Gotta run," he said.

"Hold on," Halvor called, scooting the cat away with his boot. "Growing boys need breakfast. Erik the Red never skipped breakfast when he was a boy."

Darn it! Boom sat down at the edge of his chair, mentally willing Halvor to cook faster. He tapped his feet on the floor.

"What's that?" Mertyle asked, pointing to a small wooden box perched at the table's edge.

"Yah, I got that last night at my meeting. It's an artifact

from Erik the Red. He used to keep his false teeth in that box."

Oh no, not an Erik the Red story. That would certainly slow things down, and Boom really wanted to tell Winger his big secret. He increased his tapping and held his plate up, waiting for his greasy breakfast while Mertyle took out the magnifying glass and began an examination of the box.

"Erik the Red received that box on his twenty-second birthday," Halvor said. "It was carved by Thor the Thumbless, a distant cousin by marriage who never ate breakfast. Therefore, he was prone to work-related accidents."

Mertyle turned the box over. "It says 'Made in China.'"

Halvor poured more oil into the pan. "That's a decoy sticker, to protect the box from getting into the hands of someone who wouldn't appreciate it. Someone who's not a direct descendant." Mertyle pursed her lips, skepticism written all over her.

Halvor flipped a fish fillet and it landed with a splat in the hot oil. "We inducted a new member last night. He's a direct descendant of Thor the Thumbless. He's carving a genuine Viking dragon ship."

"What happens when you *induct* someone?" Boom asked. A Velcro dart, an escapee from the dartboard above his bed, fell out of his hair and onto the table. He really needed to take a bath one of these days.

"I can't tell you exactly what happens. That's a secret," Halvor replied with a devilish look. "But I can tell you that it's an ancient ceremony from Viking days past. Every member must swear an ancient oath of brotherhood and never break it." He scratched his big belly, held captive beneath his gray sweatshirt. *Erik's Fan Club* was written across the shirt in red letters. "I can't say any more than that, for sure."

Boom stopped kicking the table legs and put down his plate. "What happens if you break an ancient oath?"

"Bad things happen." Halvor slid a fillet onto Boom's plate and leaned across the table. His belly knocked over the marmalade. "One time, Erik the Red's brother, Erik the Black, got caught stealing from Erik the Red's chest of gold. Fifth rule of the Viking oath is, *Never steal from thy brother.* Yah, never steal, for sure."

"But the Vikings were always stealing," Mertyle said in her know-it-all voice. "They invaded villages and stole all sorts of stuff."

Halvor cleared his throat and gave Mertyle a *So you think you know everything* look. "I said, Never steal from *thy brother.* Anonymous villagers don't count."

Boom remembered the three dollars, still tucked into his jacket pocket. Halvor hadn't asked for any change when Boom returned last night with the fish. It wasn't stealing if somebody didn't ask for something back, was it?

"Erik the Red was so angry when he caught his brother stealing, that he called upon the Viking gods to curse Erik the Black. The next day, when Erik the Black sat down to eat his fish fillet and marmalade toast, all his teeth fell out. He had to wear false teeth the rest of his life."

Boom felt his teeth. Not one of them wiggled.

"You said this box was for Erik the *Red's* false teeth," Mertyle pointed out.

"Yah, Erik the Red had false teeth too, from eating too much marmalade and not brushing." Halvor scooted the cat away again as Boom chewed the bland half-price fillet as fast as he could.

"That's rubbish." Mertyle sat up straight and folded her arms in preparation for a "fact" battle. Halvor prepared too. His arms folded as well, he faced her from across the room with an unblinking gaze. "Vikings didn't eat marmalade toast," Mertyle said. "Marmalade is made from orange peels and oranges do not grow in the cold north." Boom was convinced that the title of Reference Librarian lay in his sister's future.

"How do you know what Vikings ate?" Halvor asked, his chest swelling with pride.

"Because I watch *Jeopardy!* every night. Except for last night. I missed it last night because . . . I had other things to do." Mertyle raised her eyebrows. "*Jeopardy!* experts believe that the Vikings discovered North America, so that would mean that they would have eaten things like turkey, and sweet potatoes, and corn. Lots and lots of corn — hot and buttery. How come you never cook corn? I wish we had some corn, just like the Vikings used to eat."

"Oranges grow in North America," Boom pointed out. He was getting kind of sick of *Jeopardy!* facts. "Florida is famous for oranges."

Halvor smiled. "Yah, that's for sure. Very good, Boom. And they turned it into marmalade."

"Well, North America is also famous for its corn," Mertyle insisted. "So I think we should start eating corn."

"The Vikings did not eat hot and buttery corn. I know because I am a direct descendant of Erik the Red, father of Harold the Bald, father of Hjalmer the Hoarse, father of Val the Vicious, father of Karl the Rude . . ."

This could go on all morning, and something had just thumped upstairs. "Uh-oh," Mertyle said, jumping up from her chair. Boom almost choked on his last piece of fish.

Please, oh please, don't start shrieking. Boom crossed his fingers.

Halvor continued. "Father of Erik the Redder, father of Bjorn the Ballerina, but we don't like to talk about him."

Another thump.

"I need to go to the bathroom," Mertyle announced, running out of the kitchen. Boom nervously looked at the ceiling. If that green thing started making that horrid noise again, what would he tell Halvor? Oh, it's just the wind. Oh, it's just a squeaky pipe. Oh, it's just my science experiment in which I'm trying to create a sound that actually makes heads explode.

Halvor poured Boom a big mug of coffee. He never seemed to notice that neither Boom nor Mertyle drank coffee. Boom fidgeted, worrying about the baby as Halvor sat down to drink from an even larger mug. Steam swirled from the center of the coffee's blackness, turning Halvor's nose red. "Boom, we need to have a little talk, you and I."

Uh-oh.

"I know what's been bothering you." How could he know? Halvor removed his helmet and laid it beside the fake artifact. "You're worried about your father, still shut up in that attic. I won't lie to you. I thought he'd be better by now, for sure."

"Me too," Boom confessed, relieved that Halvor didn't know about the baby. But talking about his father wasn't any easier. It made him feel sad and embarrassed at the same time. "He's still afraid of the wind. He thinks another twister is coming."

"Everyone has fears, Boom, even grown men. But if we let fear control our lives, then we lose ourselves. We lose our way." Halvor's face creased with concern. "You're old enough to know the truth. The money's almost gone. I've got bill collectors calling every day, threatening to turn off the electricity and phone. The bank called yesterday because the mortgage payment is overdue. Your father has got to get back to painting soon or I don't know what will become of this family." Halvor's words rang in Boom's ears. Boom wanted to ask what became of people who ran out of money. But he was afraid of the answer.

The kitchen clock ticked and the coffeepot gurgled. Mertyle came back and nudged Boom in the shoulder. "Don't you have somewhere to go?"

He had momentarily forgotten his mission. "Oh, right."

Behind Halvor's back, Mertyle took the last cod fillet from the counter. It was still raw. She slipped it into her bathrobe pocket. There was another thump from upstairs. "Hurry," she whispered to Boom as she rushed out of the kitchen, the cat at her heels.

"I'm finished," Boom said, showing Halvor his clean plate. "Can I go now?"

"Yah." He rested his hands on his hips. "Where are you off to at such an early hour?"

"I'm going for a walk with Winger," Boom said, putting on his coat and grabbing his backpack, which still smelled like mud.

"Yah, okay. Be good boys." Halvor added more oil to the frying pan and looked around for the missing cod fillet. "Oh, that very bad kitty has stolen from me again."

Boom stepped outside to buy food for a merbaby. Not in a million years would he have imagined a Saturday morning mission like that. He checked to make sure the three dollars were still stuffed into his pocket. They were.

Ropes of smoke wound from neighborhood chimneys. Boom made little breath clouds that floated away on the biting breeze. The dirt circle sparkled with ice crystals that crunched beneath his feet. He jumped over the broken walkway gate, startling a few crows that had been perching on the fence pickets. Normally, Boom would have taken an immediate left, but he stood at the end of his walkway for a moment. Something was not quite right. The Broom and Mump houses were the last on Prosperity Street. Beyond them lay a field of grass and thistle, where Boom and

Mertyle used to play hide-and-seek in the pre-twister days. At the edge of the field a narrow trail wound to an ivy-covered forest, then crisscrossed down a rocky slope to the beach where Mr. Broom used to take the children on shell-seeking expeditions.

But as Boom stood at the end of his walkway and stared at the field, he realized that something strange had happened to it.

Chapter Ten:

A SECRET REVEALED

The field grasses stood as tall as a grown man. Boom walked to the end of the sidewalk and into the field, looking around in amazement. They were stalks of corn. Six-foot-tall stalks of corn — in March. Boom pulled off one of the ears and peeled back the layers of husk. Inside he found a yellow ear. He took a bite. The corn's juices sprayed into the back of his mouth. The kernels tasted sweet. How in the world did the corn get there when it had not been there the day before? Corn couldn't grow in a day. Corn didn't grow in winter. He took another bite.

"Boom!" Mertyle cried from the bedroom window in her bossiest voice. "It loved the raw fish. Get some more raw fish. Hurry up." Sometimes she forgot that she was the *little* sister and he was the *big* brother and she had no business bossing him around. He held up the ear of corn, but she had already slammed the window shut. The corn mystery would have to wait. He ran from the field all the way to Winger's house.

Winger stood in his own front yard, scooping dog poop. Not the usual thing to do at 7:50 on a Saturday morning. But Mr. Wingingham was a real stickler about getting chores done. Scooping was one of Winger's many chores and by far the worst because Winger's dog was the biggest mutt on the planet — a 185-pound drooling menace who squeezed out poop the size of cucumbers.

Boom leaned on a fence post, catching his breath. "I've got something to tell you. Something big!"

"As big as this?" Winger turned his shovel upside down, dumping its contents into a wheelbarrow.

"Bigger."

"Is it Mertyle?" Winger asked worriedly. "Are her spots worse?"

"Huh?" Boom unzipped his jacket. Despite the cold air, he had worked up a sweat. "Mertyle's fine. It's something else." He looked around. One of the neighbors was collecting a newspaper. Another was taking out the garbage. "But we can't talk here. Ask your mom if you can come to the fish dock with me." He moved upwind of the wheel-barrow.

"Okay. I gotta go wash my hands." Winger pushed the wheelbarrow into the backyard.

Boom waited impatiently on the sidewalk. He kicked a rock against a tree trunk. A light frost outlined the tree and made the grass crunchy. He ate the rest of the ear of corn, then kicked the cob into some shrubs at the far end of the street. Winger's mutt waddled into the front yard and left another deposit.

Winger emerged from his house with his mother pulling up the zipper of his goose-down coat, all the way to his chin so he looked like a geek. "Mom," Winger complained, trying to squirm away.

"Listen to me, young man. You keep that coat zipped up. It's cold this morning."

"Did you finish scooping?" his dad hollered from a distant room.

"Yes."

"Did you make your bed?"

"Yes."

"Did you put those drops in your goldfish tank? If Fergus the Fish dies, I'm not buying you another one."

"Yes. I gave him his Ick drops."

When Mrs. Wingingham finished zipping, she looked up. "Hello, Boom."

"Hello, Mrs. Wingingham," Boom said, trying to pick a

kernel from his teeth with his tongue. Envy clutched his stomach as he watched Mrs. Wingingham plant a kiss on Winger's forehead. Sometimes she gave Boom a kiss too. Sometimes she asked Boom how he was doing. He ate dinner as often as he could at the Winginghams' house. The Winginghams ate stuff like roasted chicken and cheesy potatoes, the kind of food Boom's mother used to make.

"So sorry to hear about the tournament," she said.

"I'm going to demand a rematch on Monday," Boom confidently assured her.

"That's nice." Winger's mom smiled and handed each of the boys a sprinkle-covered doughnut. She made her own doughnuts and her own sprinkles. She embroidered Winger's initials on almost everything he wore. She canned things that she grew herself. She was like a time-warp mom and she smelled nice and powdery.

"Stay on the sidewalk," she called after them.

Winger unzipped his coat as soon as they rounded the corner. "So? What did you want to tell me?"

Boom pulled Winger close so that they almost touched noses. "I found a merbaby!" he blurted. Really, there was no other way to say it because it just plain sounded crazy.

"Huh?" Sugar sprinkles clung to Winger's lips. "A mer-what?"

"I found a baby mermaid, or a merboy, we're not sure." He looked around, but no one was in earshot. "You know, half fish, half baby. A merbaby."

Winger smiled. "You expect me to believe that?"

Of course Boom didn't expect him to believe it, not at first. Winger was no fool. Boom tried to explain. "The fisherman caught it in his net and since it was all covered in sea grass, which is actually its hair, he didn't notice what it was. It's superugly and it has green skin and tons of sharp teeth. It growls and cries and bites, and it smells like mud. It ate Ted the Goldfish." Boom spoke so fast his tongue felt heavy. Winger looked at him as though he were looking at someone who was demented. "Have I ever lied to you?"

As a matter of fact, Boom had lied to Winger on many occasions — about the alien spaceship that had supposedly landed in the field, about the shark he had supposedly fought in the Fairweather public swimming pool, and about the vampire that supposedly lurked beneath Winger's bedroom window. But that was when they were little, before they'd become best friends. "It's not a lie. It's on Mertyle's bed right now."

"Maybe you found *something*," Winger said with a shrug. "But no way is it a merbaby. Maybe it's an iguana."

"It's not."

"Maybe it's a parrot fish. They have really strange faces."

"It's a merbaby," Boom said. "I swear on my life."

Winger folded his arms. "Swear on your kicking foot."

"Okay. I swear on my kicking foot." Boom placed his hand on his heart, then touched his right foot with that same hand. That seemed to be enough, because Winger adjusted his glasses and smiled.

"When can I see it?"

"I'll show it to you right after we go to the dock. I've got to buy it more food so it won't start shrieking again."

Boom took the lead, charging up the sidewalk with Winger at his heels. They rushed past Mr. Jorgenson's house. Duct tape now held the front window together. Boom couldn't pay for the window, so he had offered to work to pay off the debt. He had agreed to work in Mr. Jorgenson's garage at eleven that morning. That could prove problematic, considering the new addition to the Broom household.

"Maybe it's a giant eel."

"It's not a giant eel."

The road became steeper as it dropped down into the harbor. Just past the closed fish market, Boom could see the long public dock, but it was empty of boats. There didn't appear to be any people around either. He started to feel the pangs of disappointment, until he noticed that the bucket still sat at the end of the dock. "That's the reject seafood bucket," he explained to Winger. "We can take anything we want from it. It's all free."

They rushed down the dock, but the bucket was empty, except for a large white shell with a pink interior. "Hey, that's a conch shell," Winger said.

Boom picked it up. An icy feeling crept over him, like a ghost breathing on the back of his neck. He recalled Halvor's story. *All that remained was a shred of her dress hanging on the rail and a conch shell, the mark of the merfolk.*

One of them had been there, looking for the baby. It

might not be an orphan, as Mertyle thought. Its mom might be out there, in the ocean, worried. But that seemed ridiculous. Those creatures were half fish, and fish didn't have feelings. A shell wasn't proof anyway. It could just be a coincidence.

"We don't have any conch shells around here," Winger said, taking it from Boom's hands. "I wonder where this came from."

Okay, so it wasn't a coincidence. Maybe its parents were looking for it after all. But didn't Halvor's book say that mermen eat their young? What if the baby wasn't lost, but had run away from home? What if it had tried to escape from the evil clutches of a treacherous neighbor, or a mean, big-butted principal who had tried to make it go to fish school? Life with Mertyle and Boom might be a whole lot better than life in an ocean teeming with sharks and fishing nets. As he tried to rationalize the situation, Boom realized that as much as Mertyle wanted to keep the baby, he wanted to keep it too. It was, after all, the discovery of the twenty-first century.

"What are you going to feed it?" Winger asked.

Boom put the shell into his backpack. "It likes to eat goldfish," he hinted, hoping Winger would make a small sacrifice to the cause.

"I'm not feeding it my goldfish," Winger said hurriedly. "No way. Even though Fergus is sick with Ick, he's going to get better. As long as I keep giving him those drops."

Boom looked out over the bay, wondering if he'd catch a glimpse of a green head with flowing seaweed hair. But only the seagulls disturbed the water, swooping down for their morning meal.

"Okay. Then we'll have to go to the pet store."

Chapter Eleven:

MS. KIBBLE

Boom and Winger ran along the sleepy harbor, then turned onto Main Street. From that end of the street it was possible to see all the way to the other end, a mere five-block span. Beyond lay the churning ocean and the endless horizon with its ever-changing array of midnight blue, powderpuff white, and gunmetal gray — like one of Mr. Broom's palettes. The little shops along Main Street were squeezed together in an odd way, as if the buildings were huddling against the wind.

"What are you going to do with it?" Winger asked.

"Do with it?"

"Are you going to build a cage for it?"

"I don't know. Mertyle said she'd take care of it."

"Don't you realize what you could do with it? You could charge people money to see it. Meet the Merbaby. Tourists pay six dollars to go to the Fairweather Aquarium, and the most exciting thing to see there is the stupid hermit crab exhibit. Tourists would totally pay a lot more to see a real merbaby." Winger started calculating. "There are one thousand two hundred and forty-two people on this island. At six dollars each, that's seven thousand four hundred and fifty-two dollars. If you charged ten dollars, that would be . . . twelve thousand four hundred and twenty dollars!"

Twelve thousand dollars? Winger kept calculating as they walked. He added in the population of those who lived on the mainland, and then all the people in China. "Boom! You'll be the richest kid in the entire world!"

Boom almost bit his tongue. Selling tickets had never occurred to him. This baby could be like finding a sunken pirate treasure.

Boom stopped outside the picture window of the Fairweather shoe store. A pair of fire-red Galactic Kickers sat on display. He pressed his face against the glass, staring at what were, without doubt, the most cherished kicking shoes in the world. The sign read:

Galactic Kickers.

Developed with **space-age** technology, these impact-
absorbing wonders are equipped with **double arch**

support, steel-padded toes, and superior traction.
The preferred shoe of **Kick the Ball Against the Wall**
champions worldwide. **$125**.

Boom wiped a dribble of drool from his lip. "Do you think someone would pay one hundred and twenty-five dollars to see the merbaby?" he asked Winger, who had also pressed his face against the glass.

"Totally."

"Because the problem is that I promised Mertyle not to tell anyone about the baby. She thinks that scientists will take it away and experiment on it."

Winger nodded. "She's probably right. I hadn't thought of that. They might even stick it in quarantine, like when my dog ate a bat that had rabies."

There had to be some way to make this work. "But if we sold just a few tickets to people who promised to keep it a secret, then I could get a pair of Galactic Kickers." And even help pay the bills around the house and pay the mortgage so they wouldn't have to move. And buy some decent food.

"You boys gonna buy something?" Mr. Nord, the shop-keeper, asked.

"No, thank you," Boom said, taking a step back.

"How's your father doing?" Mr. Nord asked Boom. "I haven't seen him at the coffee shop since . . ." An uncomfortable silence followed as Mr. Nord noticed the hole in Boom's sneaker. His gaze traveled across Boom, and an undeniable look of pity settled on his face as he took in the fact that Boom's clothes were too small, and that his hair hadn't been washed. "Everything okay at home, Boom?"

"Fine," Boom answered loudly. "Dad's busy painting." Boom knew what could happen if anyone in town began to suspect neglect. The family could be broken up — Mertyle sent off to some foster home in Timbuktu, and Boom could end up in a town where no one even knew how to play Kick the Ball Against the Wall. That would appeal to the universe — part of its grand plan. He'd have to start taking better care of himself. And buy some new clothes with the merbaby money.

Mr. Nord nodded. "It always helps to keep busy. Give him my best." He went back inside.

Boom sighed with relief. "Come on. We've got to get to that pet store."

The pet store sat between the Fairweather Public Library and Bula's Beauty Salon. The window blinds were drawn and a sign on the door read: CLOSED TODAY DUE TO A HEAD COLD.

"What?" Boom cried. "They can't be closed."

"Ms. Kibble lives in back," Winger said, pointing down the alley. She owned the pet store. "We could go knock on her door."

Empty pet food crates lined the alley. Boom had to step over three sleeping cats and a family of rabbits to get to Ms. Kibble's back door. He knocked as loudly and as rapidly as he could because he figured the faster he knocked, the faster someone would respond.

It worked. The door opened right away and Ms. Kibble

stuck her pale face out. "Yes?" she asked, dabbing her nose with a tissue. She wore a flannel bathrobe with cat hair on every square inch. A little blob of bird poop perched on her right shoulder, and a gerbil peeked out of her breast pocket.

"Please, Ms. Kibble. I need some goldfish right away."

"My store is closed. I'm sick." She dabbed again.

"It's really important," Boom pleaded.

"And why is that? What are you boys up to?" She peered over the top of her thick fish-shaped glasses.

"We're not up to anything," Boom lied, trying to smile sweetly.

"We're *not* going to feed them to anyone," Winger blurted. He looked down at his feet, shuffling in place like he had to pee. Lying had always been difficult for Winger.

Boom stepped in front of his friend. "Don't listen to him. We just need some goldfish."

"I know what boys do to helpless little creatures," Ms. Kibble snarled. She blew her nose, real hard. The blow shook the gerbil like an earthquake, and it disappeared back inside the pocket. "Why, just the other day I caught that horrid Hurley Mump throwing rocks at a squirrel. Squirrels have feelings, and goldfish have feelings too. Oh yes, they do. They have feelings just like everyone else."

Fish do not have feelings, Boom thought. *Half fish don't have them either.*

"That poor little squirrel," Ms. Kibble whispered.

"I love squirrels," Boom said, which wasn't really a lie. He actually didn't have any feelings about squirrels one way or the other, but he didn't go around throwing rocks at them. "I need goldfish and I'm kind of in a hurry."

"I love squirrels too," Winger added from behind Boom's back.

"You can come tomorrow." Ms. Kibble started to close the door but Boom stuck his kicking foot in the way — risking a bruise or even a broken toe, but it was a risk he was willing to take.

"Please, Ms. Kibble." What could he tell her? Certainly not that he needed to feed the goldfish to a mutant sea creature.

Think, think.

"I agree with what you said, with that thing about goldfish having feelings too." The lies were stacking up. Ms. Kibble tilted her head with interest. "Goldfish are direct descendants of . . . of the same primordial ooze that we all came from. That's why they have feelings just like everyone else. Feelings like being scared or . . . or lonely. My sister's goldfish is lonely. He needs some friends." Boom waited, shuffling his feet with Winger. That was one of the best lies Boom had ever concocted on such short notice.

Ms. Kibble closed her bloodshot eyes for a moment. When she opened them her lips curled into a little smile. "Dear boy," she said, a tear pooling at the corner of her eye. "I underestimated you. Not everyone understands the needs of the world's smallest creatures. Come in, come in."

Chapter Twelve:

JAY the MIRACLE FISH

Ms. Kibble's house smelled like cat litter. And guinea pig litter and ferret litter. All sorts of sounds greeted the boys as they stepped into what seemed to be the living room, but so much of it was taken up by critters, it was hard to tell. "Wow," Winger said when he came eye to eye with a blue and yellow parrot.

"Bad kitty, bad kitty," the parrot chanted.

"Polly want a cracker?" Winger asked. The parrot stretched its neck and delicately picked a doughnut sprinkle off Winger's cheek.

"Sit down, boys," Ms. Kibble said, motioning to the

couch, where a fat white cat lay curled. Tufts of white hair covered each of the couch cushions. The cat opened one lazy eye and hissed as the boys sat. Winger moved closer to Boom.

Ms. Kibble pointed to the coffee table, where two fish swam in a fishbowl. "That's Jay the Miracle Fish," she told them. "And his little friend, Walter."

Jay was a big goldfish, about three inches long. He'd make a great meal for the merbaby. "How much?" Boom asked.

"Bad kitty, bad kitty," the parrot chanted.

"Oh, Jay the Miracle Fish is not for sale," Ms. Kibble explained. She sneezed again, then sat down on a stool. "He's my special fish."

"Why's he called the Miracle Fish?" Winger asked.

Rats! Why did he have to ask that? Now they'd be stuck there listening to some long story when Boom had to get back to the house and feed the merbaby so it wouldn't shriek and so Mr. Mump wouldn't complain to the police.

"Jay used to be all alone in this bowl, swimming around his castle day after day after day," Ms. Kibble told them. "Then one day, he leapt out and landed on the coffee table."

"Out of the bowl?" Winger asked, leaning forward. "On purpose?"

"Yes," Ms. Kibble declared, unwrapping some sort of throat lozenge. "On purpose. He started leaping out every morning at exactly the same time — right when Kitty finished her breakfast and came to curl up on the couch for her morning nap, just like she's doing now. So every morning I'd put Jay back into his bowl, but he'd leap out again the next morning." She paused for a moment to pop the lozenge into her mouth. Boom took a breath, intending to interrupt, but he wasn't quick enough. "It never occurred to me that Jay was trying to tell me something."

How in the world could a fish be trying to tell a person something? That was completely nuts. That was something Mertyle would believe. *Someone should check the drinking water on this island,* Boom thought.

The phone rang and Ms. Kibble disappeared into another room. The fat white cat jumped onto the coffee table and began to bat mischievously at the side of the fishbowl with its claws. Jay and his companion started to swim frantically. Bat bat bat. Swim swim swim. As the cat continued to tease, the fish beat their tails in a furious rhythm. Then the cat stuck its paw into the water.

"Bad kitty, bad kitty," Ms. Kibble scolded, returning to shoo the fat cat off the table.

"Ms. Kibble," Boom said, wanting to get back to the issue at hand. "I just want to buy some —"

"I'm not finished." She tightened her fur-covered robe and settled back onto the stool. Boom curled his toes in frustration. "One morning, I came into the parlor and Jay was lying on the carpet, covered in carpet fuzz — all dried out and stiff as a potato chip. 'Don't be dead,' I cried. 'Not my poor little fish.' I put him back into the bowl but he just floated at the water's surface." She took a dramatic pause. "He was dead. No doubt about it. I left him in the bowl, planning on burying him that evening after the shop closed. But when I came back at five thirty, there he was, swimming again. It was a miracle."

Some miracle. Jay swam sideways, moving only one of his little fins. Probably had brain damage from lying on the carpet all night. It would be an act of mercy to feed him to the merbaby.

"Great story," Winger said.

"Where are the goldfish that are for sale?" Boom anxiously asked. Ms. Kibble's story was stalling his mission. His kicking foot began to twitch.

Ms. Kibble cleared her throat and peered at Boom over her glasses. "There is a moral to this story, dear boy. Patience is a virtue, don't you know?"

Patience would be all well and good if this were an ordinary trip to the pet store. But, of course, it wasn't, and Boom thought his head might explode at that very minute. How far down Prosperity Street might the baby's shriek be heard? Would it carry on the morning wind?

Ms. Kibble cleared her throat. "I realized that Jay was throwing himself from the bowl because he was trying to tell me that he was lonely. As you so poetically stated earlier, fish are no different from any other creature. They have feelings. They have needs. My opinion, exactly. So yesterday I added Walter to the bowl." She indicated the smaller goldfish. "And here it is, the time of day when Jay usually throws himself out. Look how happy he is. All he needed was a friend." She tilted her head and sighed. "And that is why I let you boys into my parlor today, even though I am suffering from a most horrid head cold. I am delighted by your noble purpose. Come, let's go find a friend for your sister's fish."

Finally! "How much does a friend cost?" Boom asked, pulling out the three dollars.

"In this situation, a friend is free."

Ms. Kibble walked down the hallway that led to her shop. As soon as she left the room, the fat white cat jumped back onto the coffee table. It stuck its paw into the bowl and gave Jay a flick, sending the goldfish soaring through the air and onto the table. Winger and Boom looked at each other.

"Bad kitty, bad kitty," Winger said, putting Jay back into the bowl.

Boom followed Ms. Kibble. "If friends are free, can I get about a dozen?"

Chapter Thirteen:

DAISY MUMP

To the Brooms' house they made their way, taking the shortcut that ran behind the Fairweather deli. Boom carefully held a bag of one dozen free goldfish. He tried to run, but the motion churned up the fish like a hurricane, so he somewhat scurried and somewhat walked.

Mr. Mump had parked his truck at the end of Prosperity Street, where Hurley, Daisy, and Mr. Mump were eagerly picking corn and piling the ears into the truck's bed. When Hurley spotted Boom and Winger, he ran from the field and blocked their progress with his meaty frame. "We got the corn first," he told them, clenching his fists.

"That corn doesn't belong to you," Boom said. He didn't know that for sure, but he suspected it because no one in the neighborhood owned the field.

"Finders keepers," Hurley whined. "You can't have any. We're gonna sell it to the store and I get to use the money to buy a new bike." The Mumps weren't going to eat the corn?

"Whatever," Boom said, hiding his disappointment. Images of hot, buttery corn drifted from his head and evaporated like fog.

"Yeah. Whatever," Winger chimed, standing slightly behind Boom.

As Boom and Winger started up the Brooms' walkway, Hurley made a few clucking sounds. "Everyone at school is calling you a chicken, 'cause you chickened out of the tournament."

Boom whirled around and glared at his archenemy. "You know I didn't chicken out! I was in Prunewallop's office. I want a rematch on Monday."

"You should give him a rematch," Winger said.

"A rematch?" Hurley laughed a fake horror-movie laugh. "Why should I? What's in it for me? I'm the champion of the school, two years in a row. You're just a loser."

Winger grabbed Boom's arm as Boom almost flew out of his sneakers. All he wanted to do, at that moment in time, was to pound on Hurley. Sure, it was wrong to hit someone and there would be big consequences, but he wanted to — *real* bad. "Boom," Winger pleaded. "You'll get into trouble again."

Something unpleasant stepped between Boom and his archenemy. It was Daisy Mump. She was ten, just like Mertyle, and she was always dressed like she was going to a birthday party. Today her pink coat was trimmed in fake zebra fur and it matched her doll's coat. The doll was about half Daisy's size and she had tucked it under her arm. "I saw Mertyle's new doll," Daisy said to Boom. She pointed to the bedroom window. "I saw Mertyle holding it."

"Huh?" Boom caught his breath and jerked his arm away from Winger.

"Why does she have a Molly Mermaid Faraway Girl Doll? I don't have a Molly Mermaid doll. They're impossible to find. The Faraway Girl Company doesn't even make them anymore." Daisy scrunched up her freckled face.

"Mertyle doesn't have a whatever-you-call-it doll," Boom said, glaring over Daisy's curly blond head at Hurley.

"A *Faraway Girl* Doll," Daisy corrected. She shoved her doll up to Boom's face. "See, mine is from Sweden. Her name is Elsa and she cost one hundred dollars. Every pair of shoes costs twenty-five dollars, and she has twelve pairs. And we have six matching outfits and she came with a book that tells all about her life in Sweden. My friend Bula's doll is from France and her name is Gigi —"

"Whatever," Boom said, pushing the doll away, pushing away the desire to hit Hurley as well. He tried to walk up his walkway, but Daisy ran around and blocked him.

"Nobody has a Molly Mermaid doll. It's superspecial. It's

the most expensive Faraway Girl Doll ever made. How come your sister has one?" Daisy hissed. "Your family is poor."

"She doesn't have one," Boom insisted.

"But I saw it." Daisy stomped her patent-leather rain boot.

"I saw the doll too," Hurley said. "I saw Mertyle holding it yesterday in your kitchen. My dad says those dolls are impossible to find. He's been trying for two years. They don't even sell them on the Internet anymore."

"I want a Molly Mermaid Faraway Girl Doll," Daisy whined. "Tell Mertyle I want it."

Hurley stood real close to Boom. They were about the same height but Hurley had thirty pounds on Boom. Boom knew he was no match for Hurley's weight, but he flexed his kicking foot just in case. "Give me the doll," Hurley whispered. "Give it to *me* so I can sell it, and maybe I'll give you a rematch."

A rematch? Boom's heart soared, but only momentarily. Shortly after takeoff, it crash-landed on the pavement because — *there was no doll.* "L-leave me alone," Boom stammered, clutching the bag of goldfish. He turned back up the walkway.

"You're a loser, Boom," Hurley called.

"I'm not a loser!" Boom cried. Every muscle in his body went tense and he tightened his grip until the plastic water-filled bag popped.

"Oh no," Winger moaned as goldfish flew through the air.

"Oh no," Hurley mimicked. "Was that your dinner? Your

teeny, tiny fish stick dinner? Is that all you can afford?" Hurley started to laugh as Boom and Winger scrambled to collect the fish. Winger chased a flapping one under the tire of a parked car while Boom found one balancing on a dandelion.

"I want that doll," Daisy whined, sniffling with fake tears. "Daddy! I want that mermaid doll!" Mr. Mump dumped an armload of corn into his truck and looked over at his daughter, who was stomping her boots on the sidewalk.

"Daisy Waisy," he called, holding out his arms.

Boom pulled the final fish out of the newspaper box. He'd love to show *Daisy Waisy* the mermaid doll. He'd love to see the look on her face when he handed her a stinky, slimy, teeth-gnashing, yellow-squirting, green-faced merbaby. But that wasn't going to happen because the last person he'd sell a Meet the Merbaby ticket to was a Mump person.

"Come on," Boom said to his best friend. He and Winger dashed past the broken gate, leaving Hurley and Daisy watching from the street.

They avoided Halvor by going through the front door and straight up the stairs, where Boom dumped the goldfish into Ted's fishbowl. The fish took to swimming right away and not one of them looked brain damaged. "Phew!" Boom said. He shoved his backpack under his bed. If Mertyle knew about the conch shell she might get all softhearted and want to take the baby back to the dock to find its family. That would mean no Meet the Merbaby tickets.

No paying the bills or buying decent food. No brand-new Galactic Kickers. Boom collapsed onto his bed.

Winger, however, did not collapse. He stood as rigid as a wax museum statue. He had not closed his mouth since entering the room. It was possible he had not even breathed. He stared at the merbaby, who lay in a doll cradle at the foot of Mertyle's bed. It was unraveling one of Boom's socks with its teeth. The baby growled at the boys.

"What took you so long?" Mertyle asked. She looked a bit strange. Her face had a slightly green tinge to it. She must have forgotten that it was Saturday and that she didn't need to fake being sick.

"There were no fish at the dock so we had to go to the pet store and get goldfish," Boom replied with exasperation.

"Oh," Mertyle said, looking sadly at the new goldfish. "I don't think the merbaby is hungry right now. It ate that cod fillet from breakfast."

Winger raised his arm and pointed at the baby. He took a huge breath and said, "Wow."

"Look what I found," Mertyle said to Boom, pinching something between her fingers. It looked like a small bluish Dorito. "It's a scale from the baby's tail. It fell off. It's got that weird drawing on it, just like some of the other scales, but my magnifying glass isn't strong enough to see exactly what it is. Could you take it to the print shop and have them enlarge it?"

Boom shook his head. "I've got to go to Mr. Jorgenson's."

What was she talking about anyway? How could something be drawn on a scale?

"Winger?" Mertyle asked sweetly, holding the scale in Winger's face.

Winger blinked, snapping out of his daze. Then he turned bright red. "Uh, sure, Mertyle. I'll take it for you."

Winger pocketed the scale while Mertyle stared at the swimming goldfish. "I don't like the idea of feeding these to the baby," she said. "It just seems so cruel." She wiped some sweat from her forehead with the back of her hand, obviously faked because the room was ice-cold. Her hands had a slightly green tinge.

"Big fish eat little fish," Winger said matter-of-factly. "It's not cruel. It's the food chain."

"Well, I think that the food chain is cruel." Mertyle lay down on her bed. "I just wish we had lots of raw cod fillets so we wouldn't have to sacrifice the goldfish." Boom could have pointed out that a raw cod fillet had once been part of an *alive* cod, but he didn't. That would be just another unpleasant bit of the real world that lay outside the dirt circle that Mertyle could not deal with.

Having reduced Boom's sock to a drool-drenched wad of yarn, the baby burrowed beneath the doll blanket. Winger stepped back and started waving his hands around like a lunatic. "Forget about selling Meet the Merbaby tickets. Do you guys realize how much money you could make selling this thing to a collector? Do you realize? Huh? Do you?"

Boom wished Winger hadn't mentioned those tickets, because Mertyle was staring at him as if she wanted to burn a hole right through him with her laser beam eyes.

Winger continued. "I saw on the news that some billionaire bought a dinosaur egg for three million dollars because he wants to clone dinosaurs. Think how much some billionaire would pay for a real merbaby. You could have an auction. You guys would be the richest family in the world."

Winger was brilliant. Absolutely brilliant. That creature could be the best thing that had ever happened to the Broom family. Maybe circling March thirteenth on his calendar had been fate. Boom would be the richest twelve-year-old in the world! He could buy as many Galactic Kickers as he wanted — a different pair for every day of the week. Heck, he could build his own Kick the Ball Against the Wall arena.

"You told me I could keep the baby," Mertyle snarled.

Boom turned away and tried to find something in the room to fiddle with. He hadn't promised, had he? He had said, "Sure you can keep it," but he hadn't said for how long. He hadn't thought out the bit about being rich. Halvor said the bill collector and bank needed to be paid. It they were rich, they could buy their own bank. If they had money, they could hire a gardener to cover up that horrible dirt circle so they wouldn't have to be reminded, *every single day*, that a twister had ripped their family apart.

"But think about it, Mertyle," Winger pointed out. "You could buy whatever your heart desires."

"What my heart desires can't be bought," Mertyle said quietly.

"What does your heart desire?" Winger asked, looking at Mertyle with a goofy look on his face, as though soda bubbles were tickling his nostrils. Mertyle didn't answer, but Boom knew what she wanted. It was what he wanted too. But it wasn't going to happen. All the money in the world couldn't bring back someone who was gone.

"I won't let you two sell the baby," Mertyle declared. "Bad people will put it in a cage or dissect it in a lab." The baby poked its head out the end of the blanket and started chewing on the edge of the doll cradle.

Boom continued to imagine all the things they could do as the richest family in the world. He wouldn't have to go to school because he could hire a tutor to follow him around all day and teach him while he was kicking things in his private arena. They would have enough money to hire a doctor for Mertyle's mental problems. And Mr. Broom's, as well. It worried him that Mertyle was starting to fake being sick on a Saturday. She had never done that before.

"The baby needs stuff we can't give it," Boom said, trying to coax his sister toward an agreeable decision. One that would benefit the entire family.

"Like what?"

"Well, like an ocean, for instance. We don't have an ocean in our house."

Mertyle hung her head and sadness crept over her face like a shadow. Boom tried hard to ignore his sister's sadness. She was not the boss of this family. She hadn't found the merbaby — he had. He was the one who should make the decision about what to do.

"Gee, Mertyle. You don't look so good," Winger said.

Mertyle crawled under her covers. "I'm sick. I feel fuzzy."

Before Boom could remind Mertyle that she was wasting time pretending to be sick on a Saturday, a horn honked. Boom and Winger looked out the bedroom window. A delivery van had pulled up at the end of the walkway, and a guy in brown shorts was unloading boxes. Stamped on the side of each box in big red letters was, COD FILLETS, RAW.

"Mertyle? Did you order some fish?" Boom asked.

"Of course not," she mumbled from beneath her blankets.

"But didn't you just say that you wished you had lots of cod fillets?"

"I remember her saying that," Winger said. "Lots of raw cod fillets so we wouldn't have to use the goldfish."

Winger and Boom looked at each other and then they looked at the baby.

It smiled.

Chapter Fourteen

MERTYLE'S WISHES

Boom and Winger ran down the stairs. This had to be some sort of weird coincidence.

"Slow down!" Halvor yelled as they ran into the kitchen, almost throwing him off balance. "You want me to impale myself on this fish knife?"

"Sorry," Boom said. "Did you order a bunch of boxes of cod fillets?"

Halvor looked up from his project, which involved a cutting board and a pile of fish fins. "And how would I pay for a bunch of boxes of cod fillets?" he asked. Boom didn't need any further information. If Halvor hadn't ordered them, and Mertyle hadn't ordered them, then . . .

Boom elbowed Winger so he could get to the front door first. He had to see what those boxes contained. He opened the door and bumped right into Daisy Mump, who held a white envelope in her zebra-gloved hand. "I want to talk to Mertyle."

"She's busy." Boom blocked the door so Daisy couldn't shove her way in. Winger peered over Boom's shoulder.

"This is an invitation," Daisy announced, waving the envelope. "An invitation for Mertyle to join my Faraway Girl Doll Club." The delivery guy was still unloading boxes at the end of the walkway.

Boom tugged the envelope free of Daisy's viselike grip. "Okay, I'll give it to her. Now move it, Daisy." For someone so small she could sure get in the way.

But she didn't budge. Her doll hung upside down from the crook of her arm, exposing its purple underpants. "Only girls who own Faraway Girl Dolls can be members of my club." Oh no, not another conversation about those stupid dolls.

Daisy had never been nice to Mertyle. She and her friends often stood on the street calling out, "Mertyle, Mertyle, hides like a turtle." Daisy had never once invited Mertyle to a party. Boom knew that the invitation had nothing to do with friendship. It was part of some devious Daisy plan.

"Our next meeting is tomorrow. Tell her we're going to have it over here. At one o'clock." Boom could see right past Daisy's fake smile, right down past her cotton-candy pink cheeks, into the core of evil that burned inside each Mump. Daisy wanted the mermaid doll — a doll that, in actuality, could bite off every one of Daisy's plump little fingers. But that was not going to happen. The Mumps were not going to get the merbaby.

"No way," Boom said. "You can't have a party over here."

"Yeah, no way," Winger echoed.

"Why not?" Daisy asked, trying to peer around Boom's elbow.

The delivery van started to pull away. "Hey," Boom yelled. Boom and Winger pushed past Daisy and ran across the big dirt circle and down the walkway. "Hey!" But the driver didn't hear them and continued up Prosperity Street. No sooner had the van disappeared around the corner than Mr. Mump backed his truck to right in front of the Brooms' house.

"Well, look at this," Mr. Mump said. "This is our lucky day." He and Hurley began to lift the boxes into the back of the truck, next to the corn.

"That's our fish," Boom cried out.

Mr. Mump put his hands on his gargantuan middle. "I don't see your name on the boxes. Do you have a receipt or something to show me?"

Of course Boom didn't have a receipt. He didn't have

one for the corn, either, but both had been meant for *his* family, he just knew it.

"Finders keepers," Hurley chanted. "Finders keepers."

"Hey," Winger whispered, pulling on Boom's sleeve. "We've got a bigger problem. Daisy and her stupid doll just went into your house." With feet barely touching the ground, they raced back up the walkway.

"Why does your house smell like mud?" Daisy asked, as Boom and Winger escorted her back outside.

"Go home, Daisy," Boom told her. He shoved the invitation into Daisy's coat pocket. "And no party!" He quickly shut the door.

"Remember to tell Mertyle that we'll be arriving at one o'clock, tomorrow," Daisy yelled through the keyhole.

"I hate those Mumps," Boom said, sitting on the bottom step in the entryway. Winger sat down next to him.

"I hate them too." He twirled the fish scale between his fingers. It sparkled like a Christmas ornament. "I still can't believe you actually found a merbaby. You're not going to make me pay back the seven dollars now that you're going to be rich, are you?"

But Boom had something else on his mind. "Mertyle said that she wanted hot, buttery corn, and the corn grew in the field when there hadn't been any corn the day before. Mertyle said she wanted raw cod fillets, and that delivery van came with boxes of cod fillets. She got what she wished for." He scrambled to his feet. "Come on. I'm going to try something."

Back upstairs they stood over the doll cradle as Mertyle snored from under her covers. She didn't usually sleep during the day. She was acting stranger than ever.

The baby opened its violet eyes and raised the corner of its upper lip in a sneer. A gurgling growl arose in its throat. "Hello, little merbaby," Boom cooed, trying to pretend that what he was looking at was a cute, soft newborn rather than a slimy mutant. The baby flicked its tail like an irritated cat.

"What are you doing?" Winger whispered, adjusting his glasses.

"I'm going to make a wish, just like Mertyle did." Boom closed his eyes. Was he going crazy just like everyone else, or was it possible that magic actually existed? "I really, really wish I had a new pair of Galactic Kickers."

Boom and Winger rushed to the window to look for a delivery van, but nothing came. Boom checked his closet and under his bed. No shoes.

"Ask it for something to eat," Winger suggested. "Corn and cod are things to eat."

"Oh, good idea." Boom leaned over the baby again. It turned its green face toward him. Mertyle had put a few barrettes in its hair, and they looked ridiculous. "I really, really wish I had some cream-filled cupcakes."

Again they ran to the window, but no delivery van showed up. Hurley and Mr. Mump were still loading the cod. Boom felt really disappointed. Why had Mertyle's wishes been granted? The baby closed its eyes again and went back to sleep. "It was probably just a coincidence," Boom whispered. "There's no such thing as magic."

"Yeah, no such thing."

But their words lacked conviction because only one day ago, each had believed that there was no such thing as a merbaby.

Chapter Fifteen:

The CEDAR CHIP SEA

Boom and Winger parted ways at the Winginghams', and Boom hurried up Prosperity Street to Mr. Jorgenson's cottage, painted minty melon. A matching minty garage stood at the end of the paved driveway, and a long canvas tent engulfed the side yard.

Mr. Jorgenson's garage smelled like cedar shavings, and rightly so, for cedar shavings covered the cement floor. Thin curlicues of golden wood lay everywhere. As Boom entered, he kicked his way through the knee-deep litter and stubbed his toe on something hard.

"Kicking is what got you into trouble in the first place,"

Mr. Jorgenson pointed out. He reached into the shavings where Boom's foot throbbed and pulled up a Viking helmet, just like the one Halvor wore. The retired police chief put the helmet on a counter, then looked at Boom as if he were looking at some sort of troublemaker. Boom wasn't a troublemaker in the same way a cookie-maker made cookies, or a candlestick-maker made candles. He never actually tried to make trouble.

Boom put his hands into his jean pockets. "You want me to sweep?" he asked. He figured he could sweep all the shavings in under an hour and get right back to the mer-baby situation.

"Sweeping's too easy," Mr. Jorgenson declared. He pulled a wagon from the corner, the red kind that kids ride in. It was rusty and filled with nails, screws, and bolts. He placed four empty buckets beside the wagon. The shavings reached to their rims. "You will fill each bucket with a different-sized screw. In this first bucket you will put half-inch screws. In the second bucket you will put three-quarters-inch screws. In the third bucket you will put five-eighths-inch screws, and in the last bucket you will put one-inch screws. Any questions?"

What the heck was he talking about? Boom didn't know how to tell what size a screw was. He picked one out of a huge pile. It looked like all the others. "What about nails?" he asked.

Mr. Jorgenson folded his arms. "What do you mean, 'what about nails?' Did I say anything about nails? No. I only said screws. Half-inch screws, three-quarters-inch screws, five-eighths-inch screws and one-inch screws. In my day, boys didn't ask questions. In my day, boys respected authority. Now get to work and I'll come back and check on you."

It was the biggest pile of screws, nails, and bolts that Boom had ever seen. "Excuse me, sir," he said. "I'm going to have some money in a few days. I'm really sorry about breaking your window, but I was wondering if I might just pay you for it?"

"Money?" Mr. Jorgenson scowled. "You steal something? A thief as well as a vandal?"

"No. Of course not. The window was an accident."

"Work is what teaches a boy a lesson. You're lucky they don't have labor camps anymore. In my day there was a labor camp on every block."

The shavings had worked their way inside Boom's socks and were tickling his ankles. He reached down to scratch as Mr. Jorgenson walked out onto the driveway and disappeared around the side of the garage.

Boom squatted next to the wagon. What a nightmare. Was five-eighths bigger or smaller than one-half? If Winger were here, he'd know the answer. Boom began to pick out the screws one by one and, to the best of his judgment, drop them into the appropriate buckets. *Plink, plink.* The cedar shavings really itched. What was he doing this for anyway? Monotonous labor in exchange for a broken window. If he just sold that merbaby to a billionaire, then he could give Mr. Jorgenson enough money to buy a hundred new windows. Mr. Jorgenson could live in a house made of nothing but stupid windows.

On an ordinary weekend, sorting screws might have seemed like a necessary task, one that kept a garage tidy and a life predictable. But this was no ordinary weekend. The universe had once again proven that it wanted nothing to do with tidiness or predictability. In the same unexpected manner that had conjured up a mother-eating twister, the universe had deposited a goldfish-eating creature from a storybook into Boom's life. But maybe, just maybe, something good would come of it. Maybe the universe had had a change of heart.

Plink, plunk. Plink, plunk. The sound of falling screws grew louder. *PLUNK, PLINK.* The sound took on a familiar tone, like a ball hitting a wall. Boom stared into one of the buckets, allowing his gaze to blur until the silver screws became a pool of silver water. The pool shuddered and the cedar shavings vibrated against Boom's legs as a roar filled the garage. It was the sound of cheering. He looked up from the bucket. The sea of shavings rolled like waves as the cheering grew louder. Boom stood and watched the garage walls expand, pressing outward to form a vast arena. Tiers of seats lined the edges, reaching so high that Boom could not see the last row.

"Ladies and Gentlemen," someone said over a loudspeaker. Bright lights shone from above, and the cedar shavings blew away, revealing a spotless, gleaming floor. White stripes marked the edges of the playing field. "Welcome to the Boom Broom Kick the Ball Against the Wall Arena." The cheering intensified, rattling Boom's molars. "Tonight the final round begins between Brazil and Fairweather Island for the title of Kick the Ball Against the Wall Champion of the Earth. Representing Fairweather, Mr. Boom Broom." A spotlight fell on Boom's face, almost blinding him. He covered his eyes as the cheering shook the entire building.

"Boom, Boom," the fans cried. Boom took a bow and flowers fell at his feet. Never had he felt such joy. Never had he . . .

"What's the matter with you?" Mr. Jorgenson's voice startled Boom, causing him to stumble and fall into the shavings. "Daydreaming, I see. In my day, if boys daydreamed, they got thumped on the head with a ruler." Mr. Jorgenson dumped a bucket of shavings into the garage. Boom scrambled to his feet.

Just a daydream? His face still felt hot from the spotlight, and the roar of the crowd still echoed in his ears.

"Sorry," Boom said. The shavings had reached up into his shirt and down into his underwear. He scratched his bottom, then started sorting again. *Plink, plunk.* This could take a month to finish. Soon he'd need to come up with an excuse and reschedule the work so he could get back to Mertyle and the baby.

Mr. Jorgenson returned two more times with two more

buckets of shavings. Where were they coming from? Boom shuffled across the garage and looked out the window just as Mr. Jorgenson pulled back the edge of the huge white tent. Boom caught sight of what appeared to be a ship's bow. Halvor had said that the newest member of the Sons of the Vikings had made himself a Viking ship. That would explain the shavings and the Viking helmet.

"Boom, you have a phone call." Mrs. Jorgenson entered the garage. She was about Boom's size and her hands were covered in fish slime. "Sorry," she said when he took the slime-covered receiver. "I've been pickling salmon all day. I don't know why these Viking descendants have to eat so much fish."

"I know what you mean," Boom said, holding the receiver a few inches from his head. "Hello?"

"Boom!" Mertyle cried. "I can't find the baby!"

Chapter Sixteen:

MERMAID MAGIC

It has often been written that someone ran like the wind. This description would not work in Boom's case if the wind being referred to was gentle and billowy. But if the wind being referred to were blustery and crazed, leaping over fire hydrants and whipping around corners, then the description would work very well. And so, to his home, Boom ran like the wind. Only once before had such a force of energy been seen making its way down Prosperity Street, and that was the morning when the horrible twister landed.

In record time, Boom reached his front walkway, where he skidded to a stop beside Halvor. They stood, side by side, and stared at the Broom house.

Bright red geraniums bloomed in the front yard — in March. They crowded the window boxes, lined the walkway, and edged the dirt circle. The dandelions, normally golden yellow, had taken on a rainbow of colors, from licorice black to grape-juice purple to cherry-pie red. The colors shocked the senses — as if a passing pilot had tossed out jars of poster paints and they had all landed in the Brooms' yard.

But it was the house itself that made Boom wince. When he had left for Mr. Jorgenson's, the exterior siding had been periwinkle blue. Now it was pink. And not just any pink. Not soft baby-bottom pink or delicious bubble-gum pink. The siding was hot pink. Nuclear-waste hot pink, like the lipstick that Mrs. Mump wore.

Halvor scratched his beard and looked about as puzzled as a turtle on a fence post. "Well, I'll be. It looks just like Mertyle's drawing, the one hanging above her bed. Your father must have done this last night while we slept, to make Mertyle happy." He shook his head and put his hand on Boom's shoulder. "I guess it's a good sign if Mr. Broom is painting again, so we don't want to hurt his feelings. If he asks, we'll just tell him it's lovely, for sure. Watch after Mertyle. I've got a few errands to run." He pulled a wool cap over his bald head. "There's some chowder on the back burner." And he left, complaining under his breath that Erik the Red would never have lived in a pink house.

For a moment, Boom thought his father might have overcome his fear. He imagined him tiptoeing outside, across the dirt circle, to dab paint on each and every dandelion. No way. Something else was at work.

"Mertyle?" he called as he closed the front door. "You didn't happen to make another wish, did you?"

Mertyle nearly flew down the stairs. "I still can't find the baby. Start looking." She picked up a corner of the hallway rug. "Hurry!"

Unbelievable. "How could you lose it?" Boom asked angrily. "You know where everything is. You even know where I put my slippers. How can you lose an entire merbaby?"

Mertyle ran into the tiny living room and pulled off the sofa cushions. "I fell asleep, Boom. I told you I wasn't feeling well. You shouldn't have left me."

"You're always not feeling well," he said defensively. "Besides, I had to leave." She couldn't blame him for this. She had promised to take care of the baby. He opened the hallway closet and searched through the pile of shoes.

"I'm not faking this time," she said, peering up the fireplace into the chimney. "My arms are itchy and I think I have a fever. And now I've lost the baby." She sat down on a cushion and started to cry. Crying was the least helpful thing Mertyle could do at that moment. Had she chosen to jump up and down on one foot, or twirl like a deranged ballerina, she might have eventually bumped into the baby. But all crying did was to puff up her already sickly face.

"Keep looking," Boom told her. *Keep looking for the only thing that might save this family.*

Just as he was about to search the pantry, a scream came from upstairs — the kind of bloodcurdling scream that always came from Mrs. Mump when she found a rat in her garbage can. Taking two stairs at a time, Mertyle and Boom found their father standing outside the second-floor bathroom, shaking like someone who was very cold.

"In the toilet," he cried, waving his hands in the air. "There's an alligator in the toilet. Don't go in there. Call the exterminator before it eats us!" His eyes bulged with fear. "Follow me to the attic, where we will all be safe." Boom and Mertyle pushed past Mr. Broom and into the bathroom, to find the merbaby sitting in the toilet bowl.

"Dad," Boom said, pulling his father away from the door. "There's no need to be afraid."

"The wind must have carried that creature from Florida. There's no stopping the wind," Mr. Broom fretted while wringing his hands. "There's no wind in the attic and no alligators, either. We'll be safe in the attic."

"You go ahead, Dad," Boom urged. "Someone has to let the exterminator into the house."

"Good thinking," Mr. Broom said. "Once the exterminator leaves, come and join me." He scurried back upstairs to his sanctuary and slammed and bolted the door.

The merbaby cooed and giggled in the toilet bowl. Although it was a tight fit and only its tail was submerged, it looked to be having a grand time. "That's disgusting," Boom said.

"We should have thought of this," Mertyle realized. "It needs water."

"Well, we can't keep it in the toilet," Boom told her. "I suppose we could fill up the bathtub." No one really used the bathtub now that Mrs. Broom wasn't around to make Boom or Mertyle take baths. He turned on the faucet.

"Use cold water," Mertyle instructed. "So it's like the ocean."

Boom got a canister of salt from the kitchen pantry and poured it into the water. He stirred the crystals with his hand until they dissolved. The baby blinked its violet eyes and leaned over the toilet rim to catch a better view. When the tub was full, Boom stepped back and pointed at the water. "For you," he said.

The baby pushed itself out of the bowl and flopped across the floor. Then, with a smack of its tail, it shot up into the air and dove into the tub. It swam about, splashing water all over the floor. Then it lay on its back, its green face pointed toward the speckled bathroom ceiling, and opened its mouth. An odd sound emerged, then another and another, stringing together into an eerie melody.

"It's singing," Mertyle said.

It was the strangest song Boom had ever heard, even stranger than Winger's singing, and Winger was completely tone-deaf. People often asked Winger to stop singing. Winger's church choir leader made him stand in the very back row, even though he was the shortest member of the choir, and had him hold his sheet music directly over his face. But while Boom politely endured Winger's singing, he wanted to yell at the baby to stop because the sound was so horrible. The song wrapped itself around Boom's body and crawled into his ears. It swept over his hair and down the back of his neck. He felt as though it might pull him underwater. What was it about the song that made it unbearable?

"It sounds so sad," Mertyle murmured.

That was it. The song felt like it contained pure, undiluted sadness. The room grew dark and the air turned even colder. Storm clouds gathered outside the window. Boom shivered again. He wanted to run away from the song, to hide under his bed. The song pressed down upon him. It curled its fingers around his heart and squeezed. "Stop," he moaned, pressing his hands over his ears.

"Why does it have to be so cold in this house?" Mertyle whimpered, wrapping her arms around herself. "The cold makes me feel so sad. I wish it wasn't cold anymore."

Boom was about to flee from the singing when the song faded away. The baby dove beneath the water and the storm clouds cleared, revealing a bright midday sun. Its rays cast a warm glow upon the bathroom floor and reflected off the bathtub water. A palm tree sprouted from the toilet and a banana tree punched its way through the floor right next to Boom. He jumped aside as the tree continued to grow to the ceiling.

"It's going to go right into the attic," Boom cried.

"Ahhhhh!" Mr. Broom yelled from the attic as the banana tree punched its way through. "The wind knocked over a tree. It almost killed me."

"Are you okay, Dad?"

"I'm fine, Boom, but that exterminator had better get here soon. I think there's a monkey in this tree."

Boom released a big breath of air as he looked around at what had once been a simple white bathroom. There could be no doubt — not an inkling, a smidgen, or even an infinitesimal amount of doubt that magic had come to the Broom house.

A parrot flew overhead and the bathtub water shimmered turquoise. A school of yellow-and-black-striped butterfly fish swam beneath the faucet, joined by a pair of orange clown fish. Sand dunes covered the floor, where crabs now scurried. A gull swooped down and pecked at the sock that stuck out through the hole in Boom's sneaker. But the most amazing thing was that it was no longer cold — it was humid, like a tropical paradise. And that's what Mertyle had said, that she didn't want to be cold anymore. She lifted her face to the sun's rays. "It's so warm. It feels so nice. Won't Mom just love this bathroom?"

Mom is gone, Boom wanted to say. He buried his sneakers in the sand, watching as Mertyle dug for shells. She had retreated from everything. The girl who used to get good grades at school, who used to have friends, who used to ride her bike up and down the sidewalk, that girl would have understood that dead and gone was forever.

"Isn't it beautiful?" she asked, holding up a black-striped shell. It was beautiful. The whole room was beautiful, and all the result of a wish.

"Mertyle, don't you realize what's happening?" Boom asked.

She scratched her arm. "What do you mean?"

Mr. Broom poked his head through the banana-tree hole. "Call the National Guard," he cried. "This unseasonably warm weather is sure to bring another twister!" Then he disappeared again.

"Look outside, Mertyle. There are corn husks in the field, boxes of cod fillets in the Mumps' truck, and the bathroom isn't cold anymore. You wished for all those things."

"I did?" She started scratching her other arm.

"And you wished for a pink house with rainbow flowers that looks exactly like the house in your painting, didn't you?"

She nodded slowly. "Yes, I guess I did. I showed the baby my drawing. But I never thought . . ."

Boom Broom wanted some answers and he wanted them now. He ran into the bedroom and grabbed the leather-bound Viking book that was already open to the section on merfolk. He needed to figure out just how many wishes a person could get from a merbaby. Genies grant only three wishes, and everyone knows that one of those wishes cannot be, "I want more wishes." In fairy tales there's always a limit to wishes, and if that were true with merfolk as well, then Mertyle was wasting hers. A tropical bathroom, a pink house — wishes from a totally deranged mind. If she got only a few more, then Boom had to make sure she used them better.

The merfolk section had a drawing of a thing that looked similar to the creature that swam in their tub, only older. Boom searched the page until he found exactly what he wanted. He read: *Vikings believed that mermaids would grant wishes if they deemed the wisher worthy.* Deemed the wisher worthy? What made Mertyle worthier than Boom? He kept reading: *Only the mermaid has the ability to grant wishes. While mermen possess superior strength and endurance, they are incapable of conjuring magic.*

"It's a girl," he announced, carrying the book into the bathroom. Mertyle was scratching her back against some coral. An eel dangled from the baby's fangs.

"How do you know?"

"It says so, right here."

But before he could show Mertyle the book, someone started yelling in the street. Boom opened the bathroom window and peered out. Mr. Mump and Hurley stood below, each holding an armful of bananas. The tip of the banana tree had burst through the Brooms' roof and was leaning over the street.

"Hey, Broom!" Mr. Mump called. "This is a code violation! The neighborhood association never agreed that you could plant a banana tree. And we never agreed that you could paint your house pink. There's gonna be a fine for this, Broom!" He said all that while gathering bananas as fast as he could and loading them into the back of his truck. Just like with the corn and the cod fillets, just like with the title of Fairweather Kick the Ball Against the Wall Champion, the Mumps continued to take other people's things.

"Those don't belong to you!" Boom cried out the window. Hurley looked up.

"What are you gonna do about it?" Hurley challenged.

"That's the right attitude, Son," Mr. Mump said, patting his boy on the back. "Protect what is yours."

"You'll see," Boom yelled. He couldn't stop himself. He knew it would sound stupid but he was so angry that the words came flying out of his mouth like jet-propelled venom. "We're going to be rich, you stupid Mumps! We're going to be so rich that it will make your eyes spin and you'll wish you had been nicer to us!" Both Hurley and Mr. Mump started to laugh. "You'll see."

"What are you going to do?" Hurley asked, mocking fear. "Sell your house to a garbage collector?"

"I've had it with those Mumps," Boom said, slamming the bathroom window. He leaned over the tub, as close to the merbaby as he could without getting bit or spit at. "I want my wish right now! I hate Hurley Mump. I want you to turn him into a . . ."

The baby was clearly listening. She dropped the eel, lifted out of the water on an erect tail, and folded her arms across her chest. Suddenly, Boom felt as though he faced a python that was about to strike him right between the eyes. He moved away from the tub and sat down in the sand. The merbaby lowered herself back into the water.

Boom had almost wasted a wish on Hurley.

"Hurley Mump's a great big jerk," Mertyle said, patting Boom on the shoulder. She gathered up the baby in a towel and took her back to their bedroom.

At that moment, a universal truth came to Boom — that great big jerks don't deserve to be turned into anything else. They deserve to spend the rest of their lives as Great Big Jerks.

Boom squeezed sand between his fingers. *I'll show those Mumps,* he vowed.

Chapter Seventeen:

The STRANGE DRAWING

It was dinnertime, Saturday night. Just a day had passed since Boom had brought the merbaby home. Forget about the saying that Rome wasn't built in a day. So much can happen in twenty-four hours. Reality itself can change.

Boom sat at the kitchen table, slurping a spoonful of chowder. The concoction contained more fish tails than usual, and something that looked like an eyeball floated at the surface. Despite the questionable ingredients, Boom ate because he felt famished. So much to do, so much to manage and worry about. He was burning calories like a racehorse. It was one thing to hide a sea creature in a bedroom, but it was another thing entirely to hide a banana tree that was sticking out through a roof. How would he explain *that* to Halvor? He had tried to sweep out all the sand but had managed only to track it down the stairs. And to make matters worse, the seagull that had pecked at his sock was making a nest on top of the refrigerator with bits of toilet paper and string. Boom took another slurp, hoping to energize his brain cells. *Think, think.*

But when the dinner hour had passed, Halvor had still not yet returned from his errands. Mertyle wandered downstairs with the baby bundled like a papoose in a pink blanket. She dipped a ladle into Halvor's chowder and fed the fish eyeballs to the merbaby, who gobbled them up like they were scrumptious bits of floating marshmallow. So greedily did she eat that she gagged on one of the gelatinous orbs. Boom was afraid he might have to perform the Heimlich maneuver, but the baby managed to hack the eyeball free. It flew out of the tongueless mouth and landed in Boom's bowl.

"It did that on purpose," Boom accused, quick to notice the sly green smile.

"That's ridiculous," Mertyle defended. "She was choking."

"Maybe. But in this entire kitchen, don't you think it's weird that the one place the coughed-up eyeball landed was in *my* bowl? That thing hates me."

"She's not a thing. She's a baby." Mertyle patted the blanket. "Poor little merbaby." She took a napkin and wiped the green mouth.

Boom couldn't tell whether he felt angry that he was being left out, or jealous that he was being left out. What did Mertyle have that he didn't have? Besides the fact that she was female, like the baby. If that was the reason the baby didn't like him, then that was a matter of discrimination, which, Boom was pretty sure, was against the law.

Someone started to pound on the kitchen door. "You'd better take it back upstairs," Boom advised as the pounding grew in intensity.

Mertyle clutched the baby. "Whoever it is, I wish they'd just go away," she said, hurrying upstairs. There it was again — the "I wish." If only she'd follow those two words with something magnificent.

Boom opened the door to find Mr. Mump waving a piece of white paper with red underline marks all over it. "I demand to speak to your father about neighborhood rules." His forehead glistened with sweat. He huffed and puffed and shoved the document in Boom's face. "Rules, I say."

Mr. Piles, another neighbor, stood behind Mr. Mump and began to complain that he couldn't back his car out of his driveway because the wheels kept slipping on banana peels. And Mrs. Filburt, another neighbor, complained that the hot pink house paint was giving her a migraine. They were so enraged that they actually started yelling at Boom and shaking their fists. He didn't know whether to apologize or to hide behind the door. But he did neither because the merbaby started to sing again.

The sad song crawled down the stairs like a creature

from a nightmare and enveloped the angry neighbors. They stopped yelling as the song twisted itself around their limbs and slithered into their clothing. Mr. Mump shivered. Mrs. Filburt's eyes filled with tears. Mr. Piles's face went as slack as an empty balloon and he turned as white as vanilla ice cream. The merbaby hit a particularly low note, like a fog-horn, that vibrated every bone in Boom's body.

The only thing to do when attacked by pure, undiluted sadness is to get as far away from it as possible. That's why the neighbors turned and ran down the walkway. As soon as they reached Prosperity Street, the singing stopped. When it came to chasing people away, that song worked better than a vicious Doberman.

I wish they'd just go away.

Another wish granted. Another *Mertyle* wish.

Winger pushed past Mr. Piles and charged up the walk-way. "Boom? What happened to your house?" he asked, his words muffled by a mouth full of banana. "You can see the pink glow all the way to my house." Once inside, Boom shut the door and got real close to Winger, like he always did when something really important needed to be said.

"It's still granting Mertyle's weird wishes," he informed his best friend.

"That stinks." Winger sat down at the table and offered the rest of his banana to Boom, but Boom wasn't hungry any-more. "If it's not going to grant your wishes, then you should go ahead and sell it to a collector. I asked my dad —"

"You what? You told your dad?" Winger's dad knew everyone on Fairweather Island because he ran the island's only bank. Word about the merbaby would spread like measles.

"I didn't tell my dad." Winger looked hurt, as though Boom had punched him in the stomach. "I wouldn't do that. I just asked him what was the best way to sell something that's worth a lot of money."

"Oh, sorry."

"He said that by using the Internet a seller could set up an auction and people all over the world would bid."

Boom had been to an auction once, when one of Mr. Broom's paintings — a seascape with a two-masted sailing ship — had been for sale. Boom remembered the frenzy as people raised their hands and waved little signs when the auctioneer asked for bids. His dad had made twice as much money as he had expected, and they had all gone out to the Fairweather Bistro to celebrate. There had been fancy drinks with paper umbrellas and an ice cream dessert that the waiter actually lit on fire.

"Maybe I shouldn't sell it. What if it keeps granting wishes?" Boom asked. "Maybe it will start granting some good wishes."

"Maybe, but its not granting *your* wishes, is it?"

No, it wasn't, the ungrateful little monster. It wasn't even being nice to Boom. Spitting in his chowder. Growling at and biting him. Was there a new pair of Galactic Kickers on Boom's feet? No, not even an old pair. Was he asking for the world on a silver platter? No, just a pair of shoes. Boom had saved the merbaby's life, for goodness' sake!

"What's that?" Boom pointed to a piece of paper jutting out of Winger's pocket.

"Oh, I almost forgot," he said, unfolding the paper. "I went to the print shop, just like Mertyle asked. I gave them that scale and they enlarged it. Look, there really is a drawing on the scale, and here it is."

It was a drawing all right, but Boom had no idea what it was a drawing of. A line ran across the page with a shape above that looked like a witch's hat and a shape below that looked like an upside-down witch's hat. But the hat on top was white surrounded by black and the one on the bottom was black surrounded by white. A string of strange shapes lined the bottom edge — like hieroglyphics. The only thing he recognized was a little shape at the top of the drawing. "It's a half-moon."

Winger nodded. "It's weird, isn't it? Where's Mertyle? I've got to show her."

"She's upstairs." Boom held the paper closer. Mertyle had been right. She had actually seen something through the magnifying glass that wasn't her crazy imagination. But what was something like that doing on a merbaby's scale?

The bedroom was dark except for the glow of the television. One of Mertyle's game shows was playing, the one where if you kept answering correctly you would win a million dollars. Mertyle was smart enough to go on one of those shows, but she never would because she'd have to go beyond the dirt circle.

Mertyle lay in her bed, hidden beneath her comforter. How could a person spend so much time in bed? Didn't she know that people who stayed in bed got bedsores? That would be something she wouldn't have to fake. The baby, on the other hand, sat perched at the end of the bed, her tail dripping green droplets onto the carpet. She stared at the television screen, her violet eyes widened to Ping-Pong-ball size. The light cast an eerie glow and the blue-green scales sparkled like phosphorescence. The baby held the remote control and clicked steadily through the channels. The cable company had cut off cable service when Halvor couldn't pay the bill, so the only channels that came in were the three that floated by the Brooms' rooftop antennae.

Boom and Winger made a wide arc, steering clear of the baby's spit trajectory. She watched them from the corner of a wet eye as they moved cautiously. Boom leaned over the bed. "Mertyle?" he called. "Mertyle?" He slowly peeled back the corner of the comforter, but Mertyle pulled it out of his grip.

"Go away. I don't feel good."

"But, Mertyle," Winger said. "I went to the print shop. It's some kind of drawing, just like you said."

Mertyle threw back the comforter, scrambled out of bed, and grabbed the paper from Winger's hand. She examined the drawing, not noticing that both Boom's and Winger's mouths had opened so wide that they were likely to catch flies. White fuzzies had sprouted all over Mertyle. They peeked out the ends of her sleeves and covered her neck. They poked out through her long brown hair like unplucked weeds.

"Wow," Winger said.

"Wow is right. This is an amazing drawing," Mertyle declared. "Look at the detail. Such graceful lines —"

"Uh, Mertyle," Boom interrupted.

"The black part of the drawing isn't solid. It's actually composed of teeny, tiny dots. Did you notice that?" She traced her finger over the drawing.

"Uh, Mertyle."

"And these symbols on the bottom look like some kind of writing. I bet it's the merbaby's language!"

"Uh, Mertyle."

"What?" Mertyle asked, scratching her neck. "What's the matter with you two?"

"Nothing's the matter with us," Boom said, pushing his sister toward the pink bedroom mirror.

When Mertyle caught her reflection, she began to shriek.

Chapter Eighteen:

ICK

$\mathcal{M}$ertyle tried to pull out the fuzzies, but they couldn't be pulled out. Boom tried too, grabbing a tuft from under Mertyle's ear, but he only managed to make Mertyle shriek louder. She cried and cried, running around the room like a lunatic as she grabbed at her fuzz-covered skin. The baby flicked her tail a few times, then turned up the volume on the remote control. Apparently a talk show about weight loss was more interesting than Mertyle's plight. Boom was beginning to really dislike the creature.

"Mertyle? Is this one of your wishes?" Boom asked.

"Huh?"

"Did you wish to actually be sick?"

She pulled at some wrist fuzz. "Do you think I'm crazy? Why in the world would I wish to *actually* be sick?" She grabbed the magnifying glass and examined her arm. "It's growing right out of my skin! It's so itchy."

"You look like my goldfish," Winger said. Winger didn't usually say things that made no sense. Boom assumed that, in light of the shocking situation, Winger was simply having a brain fart.

"That's so mean," Mertyle cried, her face turning red. "That's just a horrible thing to say." But Boom strongly disagreed. Telling Mertyle she looked like a goldfish, though it made little sense, was actually a compliment at the moment. What she really looked like was a giant dandelion seed ball.

"I didn't — didn't mean it like that," Winger stammered as Mertyle started to cry again. "I said you look like my goldfish because my goldfish has Ick. It's a goldfish disease. He's all covered with white fuzz too, just like you. It's some kind of fungus."

"Fungus?" Mertyle's eyes widened and she pulled at her hair again. "I'm covered in fungus?" She had faked fungus before, but it had infected only her nostrils. This was the real thing, Boom realized with that sinking feeling that comes when the truth punches you in the gut. Mertyle was sick — disgustingly sick. "How could I have gotten Ick?"

The baby started to smash the remote control against the bed frame.

"You caught it from *that*," Boom said, pointing at the mer-baby. "It's some kind of mermaid disease." That totally made sense. Mertyle had been the one carrying the baby around. The creature had slept in her bed. No one else had fuzz.

"There's medicine for Ick," Winger said. "I gave some to my goldfish, but I used it all up."

Mertyle grabbed Winger's shoulders, panic breaking her voice. "You've got to get me some of that medicine. I can't let people see me like this." What people? Mertyle never left the house. It wasn't like she had guests dropping in unexpectedly. It wasn't like she gave parties or anything.

"Uh, Mertyle, there's something I forgot to tell you," Boom said. "Daisy Mump has invited you to give a party here, tomorrow, for her weirdo doll club."

"What?" Mertyle now looked like a *crazed* dandelion seed ball. "Here? Tomorrow? Sunday?"

"She thinks you've got some kind of mermaid doll and she wants it."

Mertyle gasped. "She thinks I've got the Molly Mermaid Faraway Girl Doll?"

"Yeah. That sounds right."

Mertyle scratched her scalp. The baby began to chew on one of Mertyle's stuffed animals. "She really invited me? She invited me to join her club?" Mertyle acted as though it were some kind of an honor to be invited to Daisy Mump's party. It sounded more like torture to Boom. "Everyone at school used to talk about Daisy's parties. She'd have party-planning meetings by the water fountain and then she'd pass out her invitations at recess. But I never got one." Mertyle paused to scratch her wrist.

"So? Neither did a lot of other girls," Winger pointed out.

"But the girls in Daisy's gang would always talk about how much fun the parties were and they'd never say why. They'd say it was a secret. One time, they all had matching flower leis, and another time they had matching purses. But they'd never tell the rest of us what happened at the parties."

"Why would you care?" Boom asked. "You don't even like those girls."

"I guess I'm just curious. It's like a secret club and I just want to know what goes on."

Now that was something Boom could understand. Just like when Halvor talked about the Sons of the Vikings but wouldn't reveal the secret handshake or the secret ceremonies. Boom would love to go into that big hall, just once, and see what the fuss was all about.

"I thought I'd never get invited. What will I wear?" Mertyle started rummaging through her closet. "I don't have any party dresses."

"I like that dress you wore at Christmas," Winger said, turning as red as cherry cough syrup.

"Oh, good idea." She rummaged around until she found the dress. "Maybe Daisy and her friends will like me, and then they'll stop yelling 'Mertyle, Mertyle, hides like a turtle' whenever they walk down the street."

But she was forgetting something. "Earth to Mertyle," Boom said. "You can't have a party *here*."

"Why not?"

Boom pointed to the obvious reason *why not*. It was spitting out shredded bits of stuffed panda.

"Don't tell me what I can't do," Mertyle snapped. "I've never been invited to a Faraway Girl party before. Never!" She started rummaging again.

Winger shrugged his shoulders. "Faraway Girl Doll parties are very trendy," he told Boom.

"But what about the fungus?" Boom asked, trying again to reason with his most unreasonable sister.

"I'll hide it."

"Why not ask the baby to get rid of the fungus," Winger suggested.

Of course! Winger was brilliant. "Go on, give it a try," Boom said, pushing Mertyle toward the baby. He sat down beside Winger to watch as Mertyle gently pried the mutilated panda from the merbaby's hand. Then Mertyle turned off the television and knelt down beside the bed. As the television's light faded, the room grew dark.

"Baby," Mertyle whispered. Both Boom and Winger leaned forward. "Baby, I wish I didn't have this fungus. I wish it would go away."

The merbaby yawned and leapt back into the cradle. Mertyle ran and flicked on the light and stood in front of the mirror. She was still covered in white fuzz. She hurried over to the cradle. "Baby," she said again. "Please make the Ick go away." The merbaby rolled over on her side and closed her eyes. Mertyle held out fuzz-covered hands and began to whimper.

"Come on, Baby," Boom said angrily. "She needs your help."

"Maybe it takes time," Winger suggested hopefully. "Maybe the fuzz will be gone by morning." He looked out the window. "I'd better get home or I'll be late for dinner."

In the hallway, Winger hesitated on the top step. A sand crab made its way across the railing. "Boom," Winger said. "If the Ick is still there in the morning, you have to get to that pet store right when it opens. You have to get the medicine first thing."

"Okay, but the doll party isn't until one o'clock. I've got some time."

"No, you don't understand." Winger got real close. "Ms. Kibble told me that if I didn't give my goldfish his medicine, he would die. Ick is fatal!"

Chapter Nineteen:

The CAPTAIN'S STORY

Boom didn't sleep at all that night, but it wasn't nightmares about Principal Prunewallop, killer twisters, or lousy neighbors that tormented him. It was the knowledge that his little sister was sick — for real. An uncomfortable feeling way down low ached, until he thought he might throw up — the same feeling that had come right after the twister. Just when things looked promising, the universe conspired again to torment the Brooms. The discovery of the twenty-first century was supposed to bring his family fortune, not fungus.

But blaming the baby would change nothing. It was

really all his own fault, he decided, for kicking that apple into Mr. Jorgenson's window and starting the chain of events that had led him to the reject seafood bucket. Why couldn't he have grabbed a crab, or a reject flounder, rather than a contagious merbaby?

Halvor came home after dark on Saturday night, so he didn't notice the banana tree. He ate some fish stew, then went straight to his room in the garage. Now it was Sunday morning, the only morning when Halvor slept in, so Boom had a bit more time before he had to explain things. He dressed quickly, careful not to wake Mertyle and the baby. He checked his coat to make sure he still had the three dollars, hoping that Ick medicine was cheap.

The neighbors had taken advantage of the abundance of bananas, so the scent of freshly baked banana bread greeted Boom as he stepped onto Prosperity Street. His mouth watered at the thought of a thick, warm slice for breakfast, but no one came outside to offer him one as he hurried by. The fruit had attracted an assortment of seabirds that didn't normally hang out in the Brooms' front yard. A family of raccoons and a group of rats were gorging themselves as well. The banana tree's monkey was sitting on the Mumps' mailbox, playing with the little red flag.

The wind was strong and pushed against Boom so that he had to pump his legs extra hard to keep up his pace. Cold air stung his lungs as he took quick breaths. The wind tickled his left foot through the hole in his shoe. He didn't bother stopping at the Winginghams'. He knew that Winger would be at church, suffering through a long, boring service in a starched button-up shirt and a tie. Then he'd sing off-key in the choir's back row. Boom used to go to church with Mrs. Broom. She always stuffed her purse with hard candies, to help Boom get through all the *blah, blah, blahs* that never made much sense. Why was everyone so worried about the next life when there was so much to worry about in this one?

Ms. Kibble's pet store was supposed to be open on weekends because Ms. Kibble took Mondays and Tuesdays off. Boom was relieved to see that the CLOSED TODAY DUE TO A HEAD COLD sign had been removed. Two customers stood at the counter. Principal Prunewallop, the first in line, held a bag of crickets. Boom darted behind a tall stack of dog food bags to avoid having to talk to the woman he had recently moved up to the number one position on his enemy list. He was considering adding the merbaby to the list as well. After all, something that spits and growls at you should definitely be on an enemy list. Something that gives your sister a fungal disease should be on the list, for sure.

Boom found the Ick Curing Solution on a shelf next to worm-ridding pellets. He crouched, waiting while Principal Prunewallop complained about the price of crickets. "Up two cents from last year," she snarled. "Nine cents per cricket is a ridiculous price. I shall report you to the Better Business Bureau."

"It's the same price as everywhere else," Ms. Kibble gently explained.

Principal Prunewallop held up the bag of crickets. "You can't expect me to pay for that one." She pointed at the bag. "That cricket isn't jumping as high as the others. And I demand that you charge only half price for this other one because it's a runt. I should have you arrested for trying to overcharge me."

What was it about power that turned some people evil? Principal Prunewallop was picking on poor, shy Ms. Kibble, just as she had picked on Boom on Friday. She could have had Boom make up his tardy time any other day of the week, rather than forfeit the tournament. But she wielded her power like a pillaging Viking wields an axe. Leave no survivors! When Boom sold the merbaby to a superrich collector and became rich himself, he wouldn't wield his power for evil. He'd open his own school — the Boom Broom Non-Evil Elementary School — the kind of place where no one's lunch was better than anyone else's and if you had holes in your shoes you could just pick up a new pair in the New Shoe Room. And if you wanted to play in a tournament, so you could become a champion like you deserved, NO ONE STOPPED YOU!

Lost in thought, Boom had not noticed Principal Prunewallop looking down at him. "Wasting time, I see," she hissed. Boom crouched lower as her breath threatened to eat his flesh.

"I'm not wasting time. My sister's sick," he told her.

"I've heard that excuse far too often. You are a time-waster, Mr. Broom, and time-wasters never amount to anything." Her enormous bottom squeezed through the pet store door and swayed out of sight.

Next in line was the fishing boat captain who had let Boom take the merbaby from the reject seafood bucket. He placed a couple of cat food cans on the counter. "There be a strange smell a-coming from Prosperity Street," he said to Ms. Kibble. "A storm be a-brewing. I can feel it in me bones."

"Oh?" Ms. Kibble asked, batting her droopy lashes. Her nose was still red and she dabbed at it.

He handed her a five-dollar bill. "Don't that be the same street where that twister touched down last year?"

"Why, yes it be." Ms. Kibble giggled, then put the cans into a bag. "I mean, yes it is."

"Looks like they might be in for another round," the captain predicted. "The scent of bananas and mud be in the air. That can only mean the wind is a-coming from the tropics. Hot, tropical wind makes the worst twisters."

Boom peered out from behind the stack of dog food bags. Another twister? Just as his father feared. Ever since his wife's disappearance, when he came downstairs for a quick meal, Mr. Broom always looked out the kitchen window and warned that another twister would come and get them all. Just the thought of it made Boom's stomach queasy.

"Have a nice day," the captain said, tipping his captain's

hat as Ms. Kibble giggled again. He almost tripped over Boom on his way out of the shop. "Why, hello there, lad. How'd things work out with that fish?"

"Fine," Boom lied. "Fried up real nice."

The captain tucked his bag under his arm. "Glad to hear it, but it seems a shame. Never seen a fish like that one. Kind of regretted giving it to you after you left. Caught that fish just off Pelican Beak Island. Don't usually fish in those waters, but I was drawn there by . . . Oh well, you don't want to hear an old captain's tale."

"Yes, I do," Boom said excitedly. Any information about the merbaby could prove useful. "What were you going to say?"

Ms. Kibble came out from behind the counter as the captain cleared his throat. "Well, I got this urge to fish there. Seemed the right spot for some reason. Put in me net and dragged it a bit. There be a lot of splashing so I pulled me net out. Then came a strange sound. It surrounded me boat and the air got real cold. Storm clouds rolled in so fast that the peaceful morning turned black as tar in a blink of me eye. Me teeth started to chatter as that darned sound came closer. I went into the galley and it followed me. Shut meself in the cabin but it found me. It weren't no natural sound. It made me feel so . . ."

"Sad?" Boom asked, holding back a shiver.

"Aye, sad. And lonely. So very lonely." The captain's eyes glazed over.

"Lonely," Ms. Kibble repeated.

The door to the pet store blew open. The gust toppled a tower of plastic pooper-scoopers and sent the lovebirds to squawking. The captain peered outside. "Storm's a-brewing. I'd better go and make sure me old boat is well tied. Good day to both of you."

Ms. Kibble watched the captain get on his bicycle and pedal down the street. She sighed like she'd just eaten a really creamy chocolate.

"Ms. Kibble, can people get Ick?" Boom asked. She peered over the rims of her fish-shaped glasses and pulled a twig from Boom's hair.

"Dear boy, you really should take a bath." She was one to talk. She was covered in more cat hair and bird droppings than a cat that slept beneath a bird feeder.

"I need to know about Ick."

"Ick's a goldfish disease."

"I know, but can people get it?"

"I've never heard of a person getting Ick. I suppose it's possible. We all arose from the same primordial ooze, as you so elegantly put it. If we share feelings, then I guess we can share sickness, too."

"If you got Ick, would you use this?" He held up the bottle of Ick Curing Solution.

She took the bottle and read aloud from the back label. "'For use on aquarium fish only. Do not inhale — can cause madness. Do not get into eyes — can cause blindness. Do not get onto skin — will burn. Do not drink. Do not add to bath water. Do not use as a food preservative, and certainly do not sprinkle on marmalade.' Hmmm. This doesn't sound very safe for people."

"No, it doesn't. Would you use it anyway?"

"As I do not wish to go mad, or blind . . . No, I would not use it." She put her hand over her heart. "Oh dear, does your sister's goldfish have Ick? And all the new little friends? You take that bottle home, right away. It's perfectly fine for gold-fish. I won't charge you for it." She pushed him out of the store. "Hurry, hurry. Don't let the little creatures suffer."

How could he explain that it was Mertyle who was suffering? As he took the shortcut home, he knew he'd have to tell Halvor right away. He shoved the bottle of Ick Curing Solution into his pocket, next to the three dollars and the lifetime supply of listermints. As soon as Halvor knew that Mertyle had caught a disease from a Viking enemy, then someone would probably come and take the baby away. A lab would dissect it for sure. The government would hide the body in that secret place in Nevada where they hide the aliens. That would be terrible. Even though he was beginning to believe they might be better off without it, so it wouldn't make anyone else sick, he certainly didn't want the thing to get dissected.

Boom ran down Prosperity Street. He stumbled past Hurley, who, despite the wind, had set up his old summer lemonade stand. He had crossed out the word "lemonade" and replaced it with "Hot Buttered Corn" and "Bananas on a Stick." He seemed to be doing brisk business, because a line of neighbors wound up the street.

"Loser," Hurley called to Boom, waving a wad of money.

Neighbors stood on the sidewalk outside the Brooms' house, their lips smeared with butter as they ate corn and stared at the hot pink siding. Some very snoopy people reached their hands through the fence to grab a lavender or vermilion dandelion. More raccoons had arrived for the banana feast.

"There's a neighborhood rule against feeding wild animals," Mr. Mump said, waving another piece of paper at Boom. He finished the last of his banana-on-a-stick, then threw the stick into Boom's yard.

Boom ignored Mr. Mump. He took a deep breath, preparing to go inside and tell Halvor everything. If only his father were back to normal. He'd drive Mertyle to the hospital and get her cured. And since Mr. Broom wasn't a direct Viking descendant, he wouldn't try to kill the merbaby. He'd probably just want to paint its portrait and it would become the most famous portrait of the twenty-first century. But Boom's father was as lost as Boom's mother, so someone else had to get Mertyle to a doctor. Someone big and bearded and fond of chopping fish.

Just as Boom mustered his courage to tell Halvor, and just as he was about to step over the broken gate, a hand tapped him on the shoulder. "Leave me alone," he snapped,

thinking it was Mr. Mump. "I don't care about neighborhood rules."

"Hello, Boom."

Boom turned and found himself staring into the cloudy
eyes of Dr. Buncle.

Chapter Twenty

DR. BUNCLE

It didn't matter that Dr. Buncle was practically one hundred years old, and that he was so bent over it looked as if he were talking to the grass most of the time. It didn't matter that he was so old he called computers "confounded contraptions," pants "slacks," and couches "davenports," and that he sometimes forgot that Franklin Roosevelt was no longer president of the United States. None of those things mattered because Mertyle needed a doctor right away. Dr. Buncle had seen Mertyle many times over the past year, and there he stood, in front of Boom's house, gumming a banana.

"Dr. Buncle," Boom said, taking the old physician's hand. "Can you come upstairs right away and see my sister? She's real sick." Boom bent sideways so he could see the doctor's face.

"Oh, that's just wonderful," Dr. Buncle said with a large, toothless grin. Wonderful? How can being sick be wonderful? "Your sister is a delight. Such a vibrant imagination. She always gives me a good chuckle. Why, I'll never forget the time she used bubble gum to make chicken pox pimples."

"No, she's really sick this time," Boom said, pulling gently on Dr. Buncle's arm, afraid that it might snap like a twig. He had heard that old people's bones did that sometimes. "She has fungus."

"Then you are in luck, young man. I have fungus expertise, having treated countless itchy feet during World War II."

"Can you come and look at her? She needs some medicine."

"All your sister needs is a pat on the head and a lollipop." Dr. Buncle took a stick of candy from his coat pocket and twirled it. "It is my experience that girls are most fond of tangy tangerine."

Boom pulled a bit harder. "Please," he urged. "She needs your help." But then a terrible thought occurred to him. "How much do you charge?"

"I am happy to see your sister at no charge," the doctor

said. "Lead the way, young man." He began to shuffle his feet up the walkway in superslow motion.

"Can't you go any faster?" Boom asked.

"The trouble with your generation is that you are all in a hurry." Shuffle, shuffle.

Boom kicked some rocks out of the doctor's path. He let go of the old man's arm and tried pushing him instead.

"Whoa, Nelly," the doctor cried, almost losing his balance.

"Sorry," Boom muttered. Shuffle, shuffle.

The scent of coffee drifted from the Brooms' house, and that meant that Halvor was at work in the kitchen. Boom did not want to take the doctor through the kitchen door and face Halvor's questions — not yet. Best to get Mertyle treated first so Halvor wouldn't have another reason, other than being a direct Viking descendent, to hate the merbaby.

"Kitchen floor's just been waxed," Boom lied as he led the doctor around to the back door. "Don't want you to slip and break a hip or something."

"In my day," Dr. Buncle began. Like Mr. Jorgenson, Dr. Buncle enjoyed talking about the old days, except his days were at the beginning of time. "In my day we didn't wax floors. Wax was hard to come by in my day, so we used bacon grease and hair tonic." Boom pushed Dr. Buncle over a broken garden hose and around a garbage can where a chipmunk was stuffing banana into its cheeks. "In my day we didn't have bananas in the winter. Everyone got scurvy."

Shuffle, shuffle. Boom considered pushing Dr. Buncle in the wheelbarrow to speed things up, but the tire was flat.

After an eternity they reached the Brooms' back door. Boom put his finger to his lips. "Shhh," he told Dr. Buncle. "Halvor doesn't like to be disturbed on Sunday morning."

Up the stairs they went, which took forever because Dr. Buncle had to stop every two steps to catch his breath. Boom kept his ears tuned to the kitchen, where Halvor hummed and chopped. One step, then another. Rest and breathe. *Get a move on,* Boom wanted to yell. What was it about getting old that made people so slow? No way was Boom ever going to be that slow. He'd buy one of those motorized chairs and get huge tractor wheels and a really loud horn and blast his way down the street.

Boom stood one step lower than the doctor and pushed his back against the doctor's bony bottom, trying to hasten their progress. "Confounded stairs," the doctor said between great intakes of breath. "In my day, if you had this many stairs, you'd stop in the middle for a picnic."

Mertyle emerged from the bathroom just as Boom and the doctor reached the second-floor landing. Fortunately, except for the magnifying glass, her hands were empty. "Where's the baby?" Boom whispered.

"In the bathtub." She shut the bathroom door. "Hello, Dr. Buncle." Mertyle's fuzz had come in so thick that the skin on her neck and hands could not be seen at all. "I'm sick," she told him.

Dr. Buncle adjusted his spectacles and twisted his neck.

He clapped his hands with glee. "Oh, wonderful, wonderful. What an imagination."

Mertyle offered the magnifying glass. "Look, it's real. I'm really sick. I have Ick."

"Ick?" The doctor peered through the glass.

Boom tried to convince himself that everything was going to be okay. He had found a doctor for Mertyle and the doctor would give Mertyle some medicine. The baby was happy in the tub, and after church, Winger was coming over to start making plans to sell the special Meet the Merbaby tickets. The money would flow in and good things would start happening.

"Boom?" Halvor called from downstairs.

"Don't tell Halvor," Mertyle whispered over the doctor's head. "Boom, do whatever you have to do, just don't tell him about the merbaby. If he finds out that the baby made me sick, he'll send her away. I don't want anyone to take her away. Please."

Boom wasn't about to let anyone send the baby away. If there was one thing he was certain of, that was it — that, and the fact that Dr. Buncle had really bad gas.

"It's going to be okay," he assured his little sister.

Boom hurried to the kitchen, surprised to find Mr. Broom sitting in one of the painted chairs. "The wind is getting into the attic," Mr. Broom mumbled, wrapping his palms around a steaming mug of Halvor's thick coffee. "I don't like the wind." The father who had often hiked around Fairweather Island looking for windswept places to paint, and who had taken his children bike riding down breezy country lanes, had been replaced by a stranger all jittery with nerves. How different he was. How much older he seemed to Boom, as if time had picked on him like a bully.

"Hi, Dad," Boom said, wanting to tell him everything.

"Hi, Boom." Mr. Broom reached out and patted Boom's shoulder. "Stay inside, where it's safe."

Boom wanted to ask him stuff like, *How are you?* and *When will you stop being afraid?* and *What would you do if you met a merbaby?* but his father's gaze darted around the room, uncertain and distant.

"Boom!" Halvor got right in his face, shaking a spatula. "What happened to the bathroom? Why would you turn the bathtub into an aquarium? Why would you plant a banana tree in the floor? Do you know how much it costs to repair a roof?"

Even though Boom had been the one to pour salt into the bathtub, everything else had been the result of Mertyle's stupid wish. Yet no one would ever suspect Mertyle. No one ever blamed Mertyle for anything. But Boom couldn't be mad at Mertyle, not at that moment. Not when she was *really* sick.

Halvor drummed fingers on his bulging belly. "Did we agree that you could get a new pet? No, we did not. That cat is bad enough, stealing my big fish, but now there's a seagull walking on the counter. What do you have to say for yourself, Boom?"

No excuses came. *Think, think.* Should he begin with the banana tree or the crab that was scuttling behind Halvor at that very moment? Boom's brain felt like a big black hole, like you could see through one ear and out the other. "Sorry?" was all he managed to say. He took a deep breath, steadying himself for more ranting and bellowing. After all, a banana tree through the roof was not like stealing a pack of gum from the drugstore, or kicking an apple into a window. It was bigger and it was messier.

But Halvor almost knocked Boom off his feet with a powerful wink. He got real close and whispered so Mr. Broom couldn't hear. "Brilliant, Boom. You've made your father come out of the attic. He certainly can't stay up there with a hole in the roof." Another wink.

It was true. For the first time, Boom was grateful to the merbaby for granting one of Mertyle's wishes. If his father couldn't hide in the attic, maybe, just maybe, he'd start to get better.

"And good idea about giving Mertyle a party," Halvor added. "It'll do her some good, for sure."

Boom glanced at the kitchen clock. The stupid party was only twenty minutes away and Dr. Buncle was still upstairs. "We have to cancel the party," Boom said, ready to race across the street and tell Daisy Mump to forget about it.

Halvor's expression turned grim. "Erik the Red will rise from his grave and curse you if you do," he warned. "Mertyle left me a note and it says that she's busy getting ready for the party, so I'm making appetizers. We can't really afford the extra food, but you've got Winger for a friend and Mertyle's got no one. She needs this party, for sure."

How could Boom explain that the odds of fuzz-covered Mertyle making friends at this party were about the same as the odds of Erik the Red rising from his grave?

"The wind is picking up," Mr. Broom nervously reported while staring out the kitchen window. "We should all hide under the beds."

"Oh, just a bit of wind," Halvor said. "Nothing to worry about." The branches swayed more than usual and the nosy neighbors standing outside pulled up their coat collars and held on to their hats. A bad feeling tugged at the back of Boom's mind. The captain had warned about an incoming storm.

Halvor poured more coffee into Mr. Broom's mug. "Yah, you just sit right there and relax while I make appetizers. A party will do us all some good." He opened the refrigerator. "Do you think the little girls will prefer fish kebobs or deep fried fish skin?"

Halvor didn't ask any more questions — like, *How'd you get a banana tree into the house* or *Where'd you get all that white sand?* Like Boom, all he could think about was Mertyle. Except, while Halvor was focused on making Mertyle happy, Boom was focused on saving her life.

Halvor found some doilies in a drawer and placed them on a tray. There really was going to be a party, with Daisy Mump and her evil minions. This was a huge risk. What if the merbaby started shrieking? Boom grabbed a fish kebob while Halvor wasn't looking. If he had learned one thing, it was that a full merbaby was a quiet merbaby.

"Boom," Mertyle called.

"Go help your sister," Halvor said. When he noticed the missing kebob, he shook his fist at the seagull. "You thieving rat of the sea!"

Before Boom ran to check on Dr. Buncle's progress, he glanced at his father. A deep longing pulled at him. But the thundering of patent-leather-clad feet on the porch, and the pounding of eager fists on the door, announced the arrival of the party guests.

Chapter Twenty-one:

STAIR SURFING

Boom stood in the entryway between the front door and the stairs that led to the second floor. Outside the door stood Daisy and her horde; at the top of the stairs stood Mertyle and Dr. Buncle. Boom's head shot right, then left, then right again, like he was watching a tennis game.

"Greet the guests," Halvor called from the kitchen.

Mertyle gasped, holding out her fuzz-covered arms. "Oh no! I'm not ready." She ran into the bedroom and slammed the door. Dr. Buncle clung tightly to the rail at the top of the stairs.

"That's a long trek down," he muttered. "Might take me all afternoon. Should have packed a sack lunch."

Daisy Mump pounded on the front door again. Boom couldn't let the little girls in and risk having them speak to Dr. Buncle. The Brooms had enough problems without the entire neighborhood talking about fungus. That wouldn't go over well at school. Nurse Krud already picked through Boom's hair every other week, mistaking dandelion seeds for head lice. Didn't need to add a search for body fungus as well. He had to get the doctor out of the house before the party began.

Boom ran up the stairs and took the doctor's elbow.

"Whoa there, Nelly. Give an old man some room to navigate these confounded stairs. This is like descending Mount Everest."

Suddenly, Boom had a great idea. Well, maybe not a *great* idea — not like Mr. Franklin deciding to fly a kite in an electrical storm, or Dr. Fleming deciding to turn mold into medicine — but it was an idea that, if implemented, would solve an immediate problem. "You can go faster if you bump down the stairs on your bottom," he suggested.

Dr. Buncle twisted his neck and peered at Boom. "Young man, whatever do you mean?"

"Like this." Boom bumped his way down and reached the last step in less than two seconds. "Go on, give it a try. It's fun." Of course, there was the possibility that the doctor would break into a million pieces, but Boom was willing to risk it to keep Halvor and the party guests and all the neigh-bors from finding out about Mertyle's Ick.

"Hey! We're here!" Daisy Mump yelled. "The wind is messing up our hair."

"Boom, get the door," Halvor ordered from the kitchen.

Boom ran up the stairs and demonstrated again. "Come on, Dr. Buncle. It's fun, really it is."

Dr. Buncle chuckled. "Why yes, I should like to try that." With much shifting and bending and groaning, Boom helped the old doctor into a seated position. Boom gave a gentle push to get things going. Bump, bump. "Oh," the doctor said. Bump, bump. "My word." The descent was steady, though still slower than Boom had anticipated.

The stairs vibrated as Daisy and her groupies threw their bodies against the door. They had turned themselves into a patent-leather battering ram. Boom slid down the stairs and opened the front door just enough to stick out his head. "You're ten minutes early," he snarled.

"So?" Daisy asked, puffing out her pink cheeks. The wind billowed her skirt.

"So, the party hasn't started yet. Wait here." He shut the door and locked it but doubted that a single bolt could keep Daisy Mump out. That little body of hers was short but stout. She could probably throw herself against the door all afternoon.

Dr. Buncle was only about one third of the way down. Bump, bump. "Oh, my spine." Bump, bump. "Oh, my gall-bladder."

"Good job," Boom said, cupping his hands around his mouth like a megaphone. "Almost there. Go, Dr. Buncle, go!"

The scent of mud tickled Boom's nostrils. He looked up to find that the merbaby sat at the top of the stairs. She had managed to get out of the bathroom!

He started to wave at the creature. "Get back, get back." But the baby wasn't about to take orders from Boom. She peered down at him and smiled most evilly. Boom kept waving. "Go," he said. "Go!"

"Don't hurry me, young man," the doctor said as Boom jumped up and down, waving wildly.

"Go back to the bathroom," Boom cried, but the baby still did not obey.

"I don't need to use the bathroom," the doctor said. Bump, bump. "After all this impact, I may never be able to use the bathroom again." Bump, bump.

Boom didn't know what to do. Daisy kept hurling herself like a cannonball against the door, and the hinges had begun to groan under the impact. That old door couldn't hold out much longer. The baby swung her blue-green tail around and sat at the edge of the top stair. Then, with a little push, she slid down the stairs like a professional surfer, skimming over the top of each step like the wind skims over a roof. It was a beautiful sight to behold. Fortunately, Dr. Buncle was too busy bumping to notice.

"Wow," Boom said when the baby landed at his feet. She flapped her tail and snorted happily. Then she snatched the fish kebob from Boom's pocket. After consuming the greasy meal, she pointed the sharp kebob stick at him. Was she going to stab him? Poke him to death right in the middle of the day? Boom held his breath, waiting for the baby to make the next move. To his relief, she simply stuck the stick back into his pocket. The ground shuddered as Daisy rammed the door.

"Let us in!"

"Boom!" Halvor called out.

Boom needed to get that baby back upstairs. She seemed to be in a good mood after stair surfing, so he reached forward to pick her up. She growled at him. "Okay, okay," he said, taking a step back. It had occurred to Boom that if the baby could make a banana tree sprout from a bathroom floor, she could also make one sprout from a person's head. "I won't touch you," he assured her. "But you've got to get back upstairs."

"Upstairs?" the doctor asked with alarm.

"No, not you, Doctor. You need to come *downstairs*."

"Confounded confusing." Bump, bump.

The merbaby began to make her way back up the stairs, pulling herself with her green hands right past the doctor, who twisted his neck and peered at her. "That's the strangest iguana I've ever seen," Dr. Buncle commented as the baby flopped past. "In my day we didn't have exotic pets. We put slugs in jars, and when they shriveled up we threw them in the trash." Bump, bump. "Oh, my kidneys." Bump, bump. "Lord have mercy."

"Mertyle," Boom cried out as the baby arranged herself for another slide. This was all Mertyle's fault. She was supposed to be merbaby-sitting, not getting dressed for some stupid party. "Mertyle, come and get *you-know-who*!"

Down came the merbaby again, laughing as she slid past the doctor. Laughing as she slid right across the floor and crashed into the front door.

"What's going on out there?" Halvor called.

"Nothing," Boom called back. "Nothing is going on out here."

Let it be known that that particular lie was one of the greatest lies to ever come out of the mouth of a twelve-year-old. "Nothing" requires very little thought when an apple soars through someone's window, or a kid blows a bubble on Principal Prunewallop's playground. "Nothing" comes easily in common twelve-year-old situations. But when a merbaby is sliding down the stairs, "nothing" takes a great deal of self-control.

"Some assistance, if you please," Dr. Buncle requested, having made it to the last step. With much twisting and snapping and groaning, Boom helped the doctor to his feet and pulled him toward the back door.

"Will you be coming back with the medicine?" Boom asked. "Or will you give us a prescription?"

Dr. Buncle, looking more than a bit disheveled, pulled a lollipop from his jacket pocket. "This is all the medicine your sister needs."

Tangy tangerine. Surely he was joking. Surely he understood the extent of Mertyle's condition? He had fungus expertise. "But she has Ick. She's covered in fuzz."

"There's no such thing as Ick, young man. School glue and shredded cotton, that's what she's used this time. Such a delightful child. It will all wash off when she takes a bath, though it might clog the plumbing." He handed the lollipop to Boom. "By the way, I found a rock crab in your hallway. You should call an exterminator."

"Let us in! Let us in!" the little girls chanted.

"Boom, don't make me come out there," Halvor threatened.

The wind rushed in as Boom gave the doctor a little push out the back door. His visit had been a complete waste of time, like making the bed, or screwing the lid back on the marmalade jar, or getting dressed for a party that shouldn't be happening in the first place.

Boom closed the back door, opened the closet door, then ran to the front door. The pressure was starting to get to him. This was really too much to expect of someone who just wanted a new pair of kicking shoes and a rematch. Way too much. Winger should be helping with all this, not sitting in church trying to break the stained glass with his falsetto.

"You're still early," Boom told Daisy, opening the door just an inch. Then he shut it again and locked it, just as the merbaby began another slide. This time Boom was ready. He stuck out his kicking foot and imagined that he was playing a game of Kick the Ball Against the Wall. When the baby slid across the floor, she ricocheted off his foot and slid right into the entryway closet, laughing and snorting all the way. Perfect aim. Ten points to Boom.

"Don't leave this closet," Boom warned, shaking his finger at the little menace. Thinking how hard it would be to live with a banana tree sticking out of his head, he softened his tone. "Stay there."

The baby raised herself on her tail and furrowed her green brow, but not at Boom. She was staring at one of Halvor's swords that was leaning against the back of the closet. Was this some sort of instinctual reaction, a survival mechanism passed down through mermaid generations? Even though the Vikings were long dead, she sensed their presence. "Stay in this closet because there are Vikings out here," Boom warned. The baby's eyes got really wide. "That's right, *Vikings*. And they have axes and spears. So stay there or they'll get you." The baby sank into a pile of shoes and whimpered.

Boom shut the closet door. It wasn't that he wanted to scare the little thing, he just needed her to stay hidden. He rushed upstairs and into his and Mertyle's bedroom. "The baby got out of the bathroom," he yelled at his sister. Mertyle had wrapped her head in a big scarf, like a turban. The Christmas dress lay on the floor. Instead, she had put on Boom's striped turtleneck sweater, some orange mittens, and a long flowered skirt of Mrs. Broom's that fell past Mertyle's feet. Sure, she had covered all the fuzz, but she looked like some crazy street person. All she needed was a shopping cart.

"The doctor doesn't believe me," Mertyle blubbered, rubbing her eyes. "He thinks I'm faking. He thinks the fuzz will wash off in the bathtub."

"This is just like 'The Boy Who Cried Wolf,'" Boom said, shaking his head. "Didn't you ever read that story?" Mertyle didn't answer. "There's a moral to that story, Mertyle. You should have paid attention to the moral. That's why they make us read those stupid stories. You've messed things up real good."

"Me?" She pointed the magnifying glass at his face. "How have I messed things up? You're the one who found the merbaby."

"Yeah, but if you had let me sell it, like I wanted to, then none of this would be happening and we'd be rich and building my new arena." Boy, did he feel mad. If he had had a big vein in his forehead, then it would most certainly have been bulging.

"How can you be so mean to me? I love the merbaby. She's the only thing that makes me feel happy."

"Happy? Hello. It made you sick."

"She didn't do that on purpose, and why do you keep calling her an *it*? That's very insulting, Boom. Maybe that's why she doesn't like you." Mertyle began to pull socks onto her fuzzy feet.

"Well, maybe I don't like *it*, either. Ever thought of that? Maybe I don't care if *it* likes me or not."

"She needs us, Boom. She's all alone. Just like me."

That was about the last straw. "What do you mean you're *all alone*?" Boom asked, feeling insulted. He tried to mimic his sister's voice. "Poor me, poor me, poor little Mertyle. I'm so sad and sick. I can't leave the house because it's horrid and scary out there. I can't leave the house because I'm stupid enough to believe that . . ." The goldfish bowl shook from another round of Daisy's pounding. Boom's anger got the best of him. "Do you think you're the only one who feels alone? I feel alone too. I'm sick of being the only kid at school who doesn't have a decent lunch and who wears the same coat every day. I'm sick of being the only one who does all the errands around here. I'm tired of telling everyone my dad's busy painting. You're not the only sad person in the world, Mertyle. What about me? You get all these wishes answered, and what about me? That stupid creature doesn't think I'm worthy of wishes. How do you think that makes me feel? All you ever think about is yourself!"

There, he'd said it — he'd said it all. But it didn't make him feel any better.

Mertyle's eyes suddenly rolled back and she fell to the ground. Boom dropped to his knees beside her. "Mertyle?" He shook her. "Mertyle?" He knew that words could sting but he didn't know they could kill. What had he done? "Mertyle?"

"Huh?" She opened her eyes and sat up. "I don't feel so good."

Winger's words rang in Boom's head — *Ick is fatal!* They

had to get some help. "We'll have to tell Halvor. I can't take you to a hospital by myself."

"Hospital?" She clenched her jaw. "But the hospital is outside."

"That's right. You'll have to leave the house, Mertyle. You have to go or you might . . . die."

She took a deep breath. "I might die?"

Boom nodded. "Fungus is a very serious condition."

"Okay," she said with a sigh. "But then we have to come right back home, just in case today is the day Mom comes back." She started madly scratching her chin. "How do we get rid of Daisy?"

"We'll think of something. But first I have to go downstairs and get the baby out of the closet."

But when he got downstairs, Halvor was standing outside the closet door, about to hang up the party guests' coats.

Chapter Twenty-two:

UNWANTED GUESTS

Wait!" Boom yelled, squeezing through the clump of little girls — through ruffles and lace and plastic doll limbs. "Don't hang up the coats. The party is canceled." He blocked the closet door. The knob pressed into the small of his back.

"Don't be rude," Halvor said. "What's the matter with you, leaving these poor little girls to catch pneumonia on the porch?" He dumped a load of velvet and fake fur coats into Boom's arms. "Show Mertyle's guests to the living room, for sure." He started humming again as he strode back to the kitchen.

Daisy Mump wrapped her arms around her doll, then kicked Boom in the shin.

"Ouch! What's *your* problem?" Boom asked.

"You're a rude turd," Daisy said. "It was very windy out there. If I catch a pneumonia, my dad will sue your dad."

"I'm rude? I'm not the one who invited myself to someone else's house," he pointed out.

"You should be honored," Daisy told him.

Boom peered over the top of the coat pile. Honored? Daisy Mump needed to take a long look in the dictionary at the definition of "honored." Clearly she thought it meant *repulsed.* "Whatever," Boom mumbled, wanting desperately to return the kick.

"So?" Daisy demanded. "Where's the party?"

"Go home. There is no party." He shoved the coats at Daisy.

"I say there is a party." She shoved the coats back, then led her followers through the narrow arched opening into the Brooms' tiny living room.

Boom didn't like going into that room. Memories floated around in there like escaped balloons. Memories of his mother filling out paperwork for the latest fingerprint investigation. Memories of the whole family playing Scrabble and Monopoly. Mr. and Mrs. Broom had shared the pullout couch since the small house had only one bedroom, and the four of them would squeeze together to listen as Mr. Broom read *Huckleberry Finn* or *The Wind in the Willows.*

After the unwanted guests had crowded into the living room, Boom slowly opened the closet door, letting in just enough light to search for the merbaby. The light bounced right back at him, reflected from two watery eyes that peered over the tops of Halvor's fishing boots. "It's okay," Boom whispered. The baby made a soft gurgling sound. Boom motioned to Mertyle, who had been waiting at the top of the stairs. "Hurry," he said.

She ran down the stairs and scooped up the merbaby. The two looked at each other for a moment, and though Boom didn't understand much about his sister, he did understand the look that passed between Mertyle and the baby. They loved each other, they really did.

Mertyle rushed the baby back upstairs as Boom threw the coats on the closet floor, hoping that each one got covered in green slime, especially Daisy's. He closed the closet door, trapping the scent of mud so it would permeate each coat. It would be Daisy's own fault for inviting herself over.

A clap of distant thunder rattled the single-pane windows. Mr. Broom poked his head out of the kitchen. "It's coming," he stated, his gaze flying wildly about.

"Dad?"

"Did you hear that? It's coming, Boom. The twister."

Boom remembered the captain's words of warning and he took a step toward his father, wanting to comfort him.

"We must find a safe place," Mr. Broom urged. His eyes

rested on the closet door. "We must hide from the twister." He opened the door and leapt into the pile of coats. "Get your sister. There's room for us all in here."

"Sure, Dad. I'll get Mertyle," Boom said. "You just wait in there until the storm has passed." He closed the door. Yet another aspect of his life he didn't want the little girls to know about. Hide the stinky mermaid, hide the fatal Ick, and hide the frightened father.

"We're not leaving unless you show us that doll," Daisy threatened from the living room.

"Did you hear that?" Boom yelled up the stairs.

"Yes," Mertyle yelled back. "I'll figure something out."

Like a sentry, Boom took his place under the archway, determined that no one would sneak by and see anything they weren't supposed to see. Daisy and three other girls sat crammed together on the checkered couch. The two remaining girls nestled in Mr. Broom's reading chair. Each girl had a ribbon in her hair that matched the ribbon in her doll's hair. They held their dolls in their laps, with the painted faces pointing out like a little plastic audience waiting for the show to begin.

Boom started to sweat. He could see no way of pulling this off. It was only a matter of time before the baby started thumping, or shrieking, or decided to go surfing again. Only a matter of time before Halvor tried to kill the merbaby with an axe in the name of Viking revenge. Boom paced, flashing Daisy the evil eye every time she started to squirm off the couch. No Mump would get her hands on the merbaby. When he and Winger sold the Meet the Merbaby tickets, none of the Mumps would get one. He'd make them wait in line, in the rain and snow, and never would they get a ticket. Well, Hurley could get a ticket, but only if he agreed to a rematch. Only then.

"Boom, fluff the couch pillows for the guests," Halvor ordered. Boom ran into the living room and gave each pillow a good, solid kick as the girls screamed in terror.

"Boom, turn up the heat so the little girls don't get chilled," Halvor barked.

Boom pretended to turn up the heat, but he didn't actually turn the knob. Why should these intruders get to bask in the glow of precious, expensive warmth that he wasn't allowed to bask in? He ran back to the archway.

"Why is your house so ugly?" a girl asked.

"Why would anyone put dandelions in a jar?" a red-headed girl inquired. "Dandelions are weeds."

Mertyle must have tried to decorate the room, because more jars than usual sat on the cluttered shelves, crammed with multicolored dandelions. A single paper chain, made of newspaper, hung above the couch. Cutouts from catalogues were taped to the walls. What her attempt lacked in festivity, it made up for in sheer craziness.

"My mother hired a decorator for my party," a girl with frizzy hair boasted, plucking at the paper chain with contempt.

"Appetizers," Halvor announced. With a grand, sweeping gesture he presented a doily-covered tray of greasy fish kebobs. Daisy and her cohorts crinkled their noses and pushed the tray away.

"My Faraway Girl Doll, Adelaide of Australia, gets diarrhea if she eats fish," the redheaded girl pointed out.

"My Faraway Girl Doll, Beatrice of Bavaria, thinks that fish stink," said frizzy head.

"Where are the finger sandwiches?" one asked.

"Where are the cream-filled cupcakes?" whined another.

Halvor tapped his heavy boot on the floor and furrowed his brow, clearly not appreciating the fish comments. "I'll just put the tray over here so you can help yourselves," he said, making room on the coffee table. "I'll bring everyone a nice hot cup of coffee."

"Coffee will stunt my growth," Daisy said matter-of-factly to Halvor, "and I don't want to grow up and be short and fat just like you."

Halvor mumbled something in Norwegian, then left the room. Boom would have bet his last three dollars and all his future mermaid ticket earnings that Daisy Mump would grow up to be short and fat whether she drank coffee or not. A simple glance across the street at her gene pool proved that.

How in the world could he make these girls go away? Dr. Buncle's bad gas might have cleared the room. The old guy was probably still shuffling down the walkway.

"This party stinks," Daisy complained.

"Great. Then go home."

"Not until we see Molly Mermaid." The girls nodded and squirmed. It was possible that they drooled as well, because a couple of them wiped their lower lips. How could anyone get so excited about a doll? It wasn't like a doll did anything. It wasn't like a good kicking game, where the players had to have skill to survive, where a hot summer day tested endurance, and pouring rain tested dexterity. What did a Faraway Girl Doll test? One's ability to spend a parent's money — that's what.

At that moment, Mertyle made her grand entrance. Actually, she had probably hoped it would be grand, but it wasn't. She tripped over the hem of her long skirt and stumbled into the room, plopping herself in the chair that Fluffy the cat had claimed. She arranged her turban and pulled the turtleneck to the middle of her chin. Boom motioned that her fuzzy ankle was showing, so she quickly covered it.

"You look weird," Daisy told her. "Where's the doll?"

"The doll is taking a nap." The girls nodded, as if this were a perfectly reasonable explanation. "We will have to reschedule the party for another day."

"Then we'll just wait for her to wake up." Daisy folded her arms and glared at Mertyle. Mertyle glared back.

"Do you have anything else to eat?" the redheaded girl asked.

Mertyle tried her best to be pleasant. "I wish we had

cream-filled cupcakes and finger sandwiches, but I didn't have time to order them." She reached forward and pinched one of the fish kebobs between her fingers, sticking out her pinky as she ate it. "This, however, is the next best thing," she lied, licking her lips as if she had just eaten a macaroon. "I have never tasted such a delicious appetizer."

"I'm not eating that filth. Wake Molly Mermaid up," Daisy insisted. "We want to see her right now."

"We mustn't interrupt her beauty sleep," Mertyle said, scratching under her turtleneck. She grimaced as she scratched her back against the chair. The chair rocked as she scratched harder. "Let's reschedule for next Sunday."

"Get the doll!" Daisy threw one of the pillows across the room. It hit Mr. Broom's painting of an amber sunset settling over a sleepy harbor. The painting fell to the floor with a loud thunk. Mertyle gasped. Another thunk followed, from upstairs.

Boom stomped right up to Daisy Mump. "That was my mom's favorite painting," he angrily told her.

"So what? I've seen better paintings on fire hydrants." Daisy stood on the couch, eye to eye with Boom. "My mom says that paintings of the ocean are boring."

"They're not boring," Mertyle cried. "They're beautiful. My dad's a master."

"My mom says that your dad is washed up."

Boom heard a scurrying sound and turned to find Mertyle charging at Daisy. She wasn't moving very fast because of the extra-long skirt. He actually had to hold her back. She was crazed with anger. He understood crazed with anger.

Another thump sounded from upstairs.

"I've got an idea. Let's go up to Mertyle's room to see the doll," Daisy said, shoving her stout self off the couch.

"No!" Boom and Mertyle cried. Boom felt as though the painting wasn't the only thing that would come crashing down — like the moment before a pot boils over and scalds the cook. All faces turned to the ceiling as the thumping continued. What the heck was that baby doing now — swinging from the curtains?

"Boom," Mertyle insisted. "It would be rude of me to leave my guests. Please go get the doll."

"Doll?" The fuzz had obviously gone to Mertyle's brain. *Sure, no problem,* he thought. *I'll just go upstairs and get a doll that . . . DOESN'T EXIST.* What a day. Totally nuts.

He stomped upstairs, conjuring a plan along the way. He'd pretend to look for the doll and then tell everyone it had been stolen. The girls would leave, Halvor would take Mertyle to the hospital, and Boom and Winger would start making the tickets. And when the storm passed, Mr. Broom would come out of the closet.

Boom paced a bit just inside the bedroom door, guessing at the amount of time needed to pretend to look for something that didn't exist. A gust of cold air hit him in the back of his neck. Why was the bedroom window open? He went to close it but tripped over something that lay on the floor next to Mertyle's bed. He picked it up and found himself staring into the painted green eyes of a doll with long black hair and a fabric tail. A tag read, MOLLY MERMAID. That reject fish had granted another one of Mertyle's wishes. Boom squeezed the doll as hard as he could, hoping its head might pop off. He thought about kicking it out the window, until he noticed that green slime covered the windowsill.

Peering out the window, Boom found a ladder propped against the outer wall. Hurley Mump was at the bottom of the very same ladder. Boom's eyes focused like individual magnifying glasses on Hurley's feet, drawn there by a pair of brand-new fire-red Galactic Kickers. Boom's heart skipped a beat as he felt, like so many times before, a wave of despair and outrage. He slammed his fist on the windowsill, spraying green slime onto his face. Life was completely unfair. The universe didn't give a hoot about Boom Broom.

Only after Hurley had jumped over the broken gate did Boom realize that his obnoxious neighbor was carrying something. A shimmer of blue-green tail poked out from beneath Hurley's elbow.

Chapter Twenty-three:

HURLEY MUMP

Boom flew out his front door like the wind — a crazed wind that kicked up dirt and terrified neighborhood cats and made a howling sound that sounded something like *I'm going to kiiiiiiiiill you, Hurley Muuuuuump.*

He leapt over the broken gate, snaked around Dr. Buncle, and narrowly avoided what would have been a painful slip on a banana peel. A family of squirrels chirped at him, their cheeks fat with banana meat. A dog, chewing on a salty corncob, growled as Boom jumped over its tail. He almost bumped into a delivery guy who was unloading boxes labeled CREAM-FILLED CUPCAKES, and FINGER SAND-WICHES. Another wish!

Hurley ran up the Mumps' driveway. Those Galactic Kickers gave Hurley a major advantage, what with their arch support and spring-loaded soles. "Huuuuuurley!" Hurley moved, once again, to the number one position on Boom's enemy list.

Hurley picked up speed, rounding the corner of his house into his backyard. Boom ran past the Mumps' vanilla-white picket fence and across their artificial turf. He had never been in the Mumps' yard before. All those years of living across the street and the Mumps had never said, *Hey, come on over for some popcorn* or *Hey, we just inflated the pool, so come on over for a dip.*

Boom turned the corner and stood in the Mumps' back-yard. It was neat and tidy, with a stand of shiny yard tools and a row of perfectly coiled garden hoses. Two ceramic gnomes sat beneath a blue birdbath. But no thieving blond-haired boy could be seen.

Where had he gone? Darn it! Hurley Mump was going to ruin everything, as usual. Once Hurley realized that he had stolen the most amazing discovery of the twenty-first century, which would be any minute now, he'd tell the world. He'd sell the merbaby and make a fortune. He wouldn't care that Mertyle loved the baby or that the baby loved her. He wouldn't care that in a few days the bill collector would be back at the Brooms' house. And once again, Hurley would get all the glory.

Boom was about to open the garage door when a shriek filled the air. At first he thought it was the merbaby's shriek because it almost burst his eardrums. But this shriek didn't have the same blood-chilling effect. It didn't feel like a knife thrusting through Boom's skull. Boom looked across the yard to the garden shed, from which another shriek issued forth. He opened the shed door to find Hurley Mump holding out a bleeding hand. "It bit me," he cried, tears pooling along the ridges of his beady eyes.

The baby lay in a wheelbarrow, hissing and growling and spewing foam like a rabid dog. Hurley backed up against the potting bench, shaking. Boom knew just how he felt. When in viper mode, that baby could scare the fangs off a vampire.

"Th-th-that's no doll," Hurley stuttered. Brilliant observation. "Wh-wh-what is it?"

Boom slowly edged his way toward his archenemy, careful not to make any sudden movements. The baby continued to hiss. No way was he going to tell Hurley the truth. "It's an alien from outer space. It's evil, that's what it is. And it eats human flesh."

Hurley gasped. "Why are you keeping an alien in your bedroom?" The baby raised herself up on her tail, but Boom couldn't tell which one of them she was going to spit at.

"It used mind control on me," Boom said. "And if you tell anyone about the alien, then it will control your mind as well." That didn't sound threatening enough. "If you tell anyone, it will suck out your brain." Hurley would understand brain-sucking because all the boys in their class had once sneaked into the Fairweather movie theater to watch an old black-and-white movie about some aliens that sucked out people's brains.

"Get it out of here." Hurley climbed over a pile of clay pots in an attempt to get away.

"Baby," Boom cooed, holding out his arms. The merbaby eyed him suspiciously, her upper lip vibrating in a snarl. "I'm going to take you back to Mertyle. To *Mertyle*." That seemed to do the trick. The baby lowered herself and closed her mouth. When Boom took a step forward, she growled a little. "To *Mertyle*," he said again. "*Mertyle*."

With all the courage he could muster in the world, more courage than facing Principal Prunewallop, more courage than his first loop-the-loop roller coaster, more courage than that first step taken beyond the dirt circle, he slid his hands under the baby's tail and scooped her up in his arms. They looked at each other — the baby all squinty and rigid, Boom sweating like a nervous snake wrangler. "To *Mertyle*," he said again.

"Hey," Hurley said from the corner of the shed. "Now that I think about it, that thing looks kind of like a —"

"Do you have any idea how painful it is to have your brain sucked?" Boom asked. "Tell no one!" He thrust the baby toward Hurley. Right on cue she bared her razor-sharp teeth. Smart little thing.

Boom ran from the shed, but he had to hide behind the Mumps' garbage cans because Daisy and her cohorts were crossing the street, stuffing their faces with cream-filled cupcakes and finger sandwiches. The wind rattled the cans so he couldn't hear what they were saying until they passed by. "I couldn't believe it when Mertyle the Turtle's scarf fell off," Daisy said. "Did you see how horrid her hair looked? They can't afford good shampoo." The girls giggled. "And why was her dad sitting in the closet? So weird."

Even in his old sneakers that had neither arch support nor space-age traction, Boom managed to get back to his walkway before anyone noticed the creature tucked in his arms. Mr. Mump backed his truck next to the delivery van, almost running a few neighbors over in his attempt to claim all the delicious loot. Winger ran down the sidewalk in his Sunday suit. "What are you doing with that thing out here?" he asked. "Are you psychotic?"

"I'll explain later," Boom said. "Just help me sneak it back upstairs so Halvor doesn't see it." Winger held the ladder as Boom struggled up, one-handed. The baby growled a few more times but clung tightly to Boom's shirt. "I don't suppose you care that I saved your life, *again*," Boom grumbled as he climbed. "I don't suppose saving your life, *for a second time*, means anything to you." Just a few more rungs and they'd be at the bedroom window. "Why do you grant all her stupid wishes when you could grant the one wish that matters the most? Why don't you make the fungus go away?" The baby looked over Boom's shoulder and whimpered as they climbed higher.

As soon as they reached the windowsill, the baby leapt

from Boom's arms and landed on the pink comforter. Boom tumbled over the windowsill and fell onto the carpet, with Winger close behind.

"Hello, boys," Halvor said.

Boom and Winger looked up from the carpet to find Halvor holding Mertyle's turban. Mertyle sat in all her fuzzy glory, on the edge of her bed, crying.

"Somebody had better tell me what's going on around here, for sure!"

Chapter Twenty-four:

The MERFOLK'S CURSE

Anyone who has kept a secret for a very long time knows how exhausting a task it can be. Sometimes the secret percolates like Halvor's coffee, trying to bubble its way out. Sometimes the secret is heavy like a box of raw cod fillets, weighing down the limbs of its carrier. Sometimes it curdles in the stomach like bad fish stew. Even though Boom had held his secret for only two days, he felt immense relief when he told it to Halvor — like going to the bathroom after a really long movie.

Halvor listened, eyeing the merbaby now and then. Since he was wearing an apron and no Viking helmet, and carrying a wooden spoon rather than an axe, the baby paid him no mind. She lay curled in Mertyle's lap, chewing on the hem of the striped turtleneck.

Boom told it all, from the red circle on his calendar, to kicking an apple through Mr. Jorgenson's window. From giving seven dollars to Winger, to fetching the fish from the reject seafood bucket. From the cornfield, to the pet store, to Hurley's theft, he spoke as fast as he could, barely breathing between words as fuzz sprouted from the tip of Mertyle's nose.

Halvor took the story in, with no signs of disbelief. After all, he already believed in the existence of merfolk because if Vikings had said they were real, it had to be true.

"Then we climbed back up the ladder and here we are," Boom explained, almost passing out from lack of oxygen. What would Halvor say? He didn't seem concerned about the fact that a sworn Viking enemy lay just a few feet away. Instead, he directed his worried glances at Mertyle, who scratched and moaned like a flea-bitten dog.

Halvor put down the wooden spoon and drummed his fingers on his belly. "It's a dire situation, for sure," he told the three children. "You've been messing with a merbaby and the curse is upon you."

"Curse?" Mertyle asked through fuzzy lips.

"Haven't I ever told you the story of Erik the Red's first-born daughter?" The kids shook their heads. Halvor sat down in the desk chair and rested his hands on his knees — his storytelling posture. "The firstborn daughter of Erik the Red was also named Mertyle, for sure," he said. "It was her mother who had been taken by the merfolk on that dark night when she strolled the deck of Erik's boat. Taken and drowned in the sea and never seen again. Yah, that was the day that Erik the Red cursed all the merfolk." The baby had fallen asleep in Mertyle's lap and was snoring like a motorboat.

"Firstborn daughter Mertyle was just a babe at the time of her mother's murder, and was raised to hate the merfolk. Every night before going to bed, she asked the gods to turn the seas boiling hot and cook all the merfolk to death. She did this faithfully because she was a good daughter, for sure."

"Boil them?" Winger asked.

"That's horrid," said Mertyle.

Boom remembered the times when Halvor had cooked crabs in boiling water, dropping them in as they wiggled and snapped their claws. They stopped moving as soon as the heat overtook them and their shells turned bright red. Halvor always said the crabs couldn't feel anything, but Boom wasn't so sure. Boiling water had to feel terrible.

"Yah, well it's also horrid to take someone's wife from the bow of a ship and drown her," Halvor pointed out, defending his ancestor. Boom had to agree.

"On her ninth birthday," Halvor continued, "Mertyle was playing at the edge of the sea when she heard a strange noise, a sad sound she had never heard before. She followed the sound and found, wedged between two rocks, a small creature with a human body and a fish tail. It was a merbaby, just like the one here in this room, for sure. It struggled to free itself but it had injured its tail. Mertyle knew she was forbidden to help the creature. She knew that she should have gone straight home and told her father and uncles, who would have killed the merbaby on the spot. But she didn't. She took the baby to a cave not far from Erik the Red's house. She tended to the tail and fed the baby small herring that she caught herself with a net. She'd run home to do her chores and help with her little sisters, and then run back to the cave to check on the forbidden guest.

"But as the merbaby's tail began to heal, Mertyle fell gravely ill. Erik the Red called the healer to the village, but he could find no cure for the strange white plant that grew all over Mertyle's body."

Boom stared at his sister. Her eyes drooped strangely. He had never put any faith in the old Viking stories. He thought they were crazy myths told by a crazy old man. But there sat Mertyle, just like firstborn Mertyle, with a strange white plant growing on her.

Mertyle's pink walls cast an eerie glow on Halvor as he spoke. "The healer told the villagers that Mertyle was covered with the curse of the merfolk, a curse that befalls anyone who takes and keeps a mermaid's child. The only cure was for Mertyle to return the baby to its mother. A mother's love, be she human or mermaid, lioness or cow, is one of the strongest forces on the planet."

Not stronger than a twister, Boom thought.

"Don't mess with a mother's love, for sure," Halvor said.

"But Mertyle wasn't messing with anyone. She didn't take the baby. I did," Boom pointed out.

"It was a fisherman who caught the baby in the first place," Winger defended. "This is all his fault."

"But I'm the one who wanted to keep it," Mertyle confessed in a fuzzy voice. "I'm the one who wanted to make it my own."

Halvor nodded. "Yah, so you are the one who is cursed, just like firstborn Mertyle."

"What happened to firstborn Mertyle?" Boom asked. "How'd she get rid of the fuzz?"

"I don't think you children should hear that part of the story. It's a bit . . . unpleasant." Unpleasant? This, coming from the man who told stories of Viking pillage and plunder, of beheadings and gorings that his ancestors had practiced on a daily basis.

"Tell us," Mertyle insisted. "I must know." She wanted to face the truth. It was almost unbelievable — but so was everything else lately.

"Very well." Halvor cleared his throat and the three children leaned forward. "Erik the Red refused to listen to the healer. He hated the merfolk so deeply that he forbade anyone to return the merbaby to the sea. You must under-stand that he thought of the baby as vermin, as an inhuman beast. He ended its life with his own hands. I'm afraid to say that Mertyle succumbed to the fuzz and didn't live to see another year."

Each of the kids took in a slow, deep breath as the baby snored. Firstborn Mertyle had died from a mother's curse. Boom was starting to understand. The baby had no part in giving Mertyle this disease, so it had no part in taking the disease away. It hadn't granted Mertyle's wish about getting better because it couldn't, not because it didn't want to. The curse could be lifted only by its mother.

"You have to give it up," Boom told his sister.

"Give her up?" Mertyle's shoulders drooped, and if Boom could have seen her expression through all that fuzz, he guessed he would have seen one of extreme sadness. "I have to give her back to her mother?"

"That's impossible," Winger stated. "We don't know where to find her mother. No one knows where to find a mermaid."

Boom felt a rush of shame. He reached under his bed and took out the conch shell. "I found it on the dock," he explained. The baby opened her eyes as if she sensed the shell's sudden appearance. She sat up in Mertyle's lap and held out her green hands.

"The mark of the merfolk," Halvor whispered as the baby took the shell. "When the merfolk drowned Erik the Red's wife, they left a conch shell behind. It is their mark — their calling card, for sure."

"I found it in the same place I found the baby," Boom said. "I think its mother must have been looking for it."

"You knew her mother was looking?" Mertyle asked. "Oh, Boom, why didn't you tell me?"

"Because you wanted to keep it so bad," he answered. "Because you were always so sad, and you said you felt all alone. I wanted to sell tickets to see the merbaby so that we could get rid of the bill collector and so we could get a brain doctor to help you and Dad. And . . ." Here came the part that made him feel ashamed. "And I also wanted to sell tickets so I could buy those Galactic Kickers in the shoe store and so I could build a Kick the Ball Against the Wall arena."

Boom felt certain that his own greed had led to all this. "I didn't know you'd get sick, Mertyle. I'm sorry." He sat back down on the bed, and Winger patted him on the back, the way a good friend should. The most amazing discovery of the twenty-first century had turned out to be a real dud, like a firecracker that promises shooting stars and swirling stripes but ends up fizzling out on the concrete.

"Wait! That shell is a sign of hope!" Halvor exclaimed, rising from the desk chair. "She's out there somewhere and we've got to find her. The mother can lift the curse and save Mertyle's life."

"We should go back to the dock and look," Winger suggested.

"I'll do it right now," Boom said. "But what if she's not there?"

The merbaby grunted, then pointed at the shell's pink lip. She held the shell out, grunting again. Boom cautiously leaned forward and peered inside the shell, not certain if she was trying to show him something or if she was going to hit him over the head with it. A series of markings were etched into the smooth surface. He had been in such a hurry to hide the shell, he hadn't noticed the markings. He grabbed the magnifying glass from Mertyle's desk and held it above the shell.

The markings looked familiar. "Where's that piece of paper from the print shop?" Boom asked. Mertyle slowly raised her arm, as if it weighed a ton, and pointed to her desk drawer. Boom pulled out the paper and looked again at the strange drawing. Exactly like the etching on the conch shell. What could it be? The crescent moon hung in the night sky above something shaped like a witch's hat. The hat also lay below like . . . like a reflection. A reflection in water. Boom's eyes widened.

Think, think. The witch's hat was an island and the moon was casting the island's reflection into the sea. An island drawn not from a bird's-eye view but from a water-level view — the view of a mermaid.

"Mertyle, what's wrong?" Halvor asked abruptly. Mertyle lay on the bed with the baby at her side. She was breathing kind of funny, as though she were underwater.

"I'm so tired," she murmured.

"We must hurry!" Boom exclaimed, waving the map in the air.

Winger jumped to his feet. "Yes, we must hurry. Hurry where?"

"It's a map," Boom said. He pointed to the island. "If the mother isn't at the dock, then this is where we need to go."

Chapter Twenty-five:

The SONS of the VIKINGS

Boom and Winger sat on a bench in the entryway of the cedar lodge where the Sons of the Vikings held their meetings. So much nervous energy flowed from the boys that the bench actually grew warm. This was not one of their usual errands or chores. This was not about running to the market or scooping cucumber-sized poop. This was a mission of life or death.

Two hours earlier, Winger had called his mother to get permission to spend the night at Boom's. He had assured her that he would get to bed early since the next day was a school day. Winger didn't usually lie to his mother, but sometimes, in matters of life and death, stretching the truth is necessary. Leaving Mertyle at the house, Boom, Winger, and Halvor had headed to the dock with the baby tucked in a laundry basket. No mercreatures were found, no conch shells, either, so Halvor insisted that they follow him to the lodge.

Finally, Boom would find out what went on at a secret Viking meeting. Halvor had ordered them not to move from the entryway bench until someone called them into the hall. Non-members weren't usually allowed in the great hall, except during holiday dances. Boom reached down and touched the edge of the laundry basket, where the baby lay hidden beneath a blanket. She had peered out when they'd first entered the lodge, but upon seeing the array of ancient weaponry hanging in the entryway, she had burrowed deep and had remained still ever since.

A large bronze plaque hung on the wall across from the bench. It read:

Oath of the Sons of the Vikings

If thy brother is hungry, fish for him.
If thy brother is cold, build shelter for him.
If thy brother is sick, tend to him.
If thy brother is lost, help him find his way.
Never steal from thy brother.

Cars were pulling up to the entryway, and men rushed in, mumbling about "an emergency meeting" and "unseasonably strong wind." They wore overcoats and snow parkas, and a few came in bathrobes. One guy wore a pair of fuzzy bunny slippers. Some carried entire plates of food — others, just a drumstick or a roll from their interrupted Sunday night dinners. Mr. Jorgenson, the retired chief of police, stopped to glare at Boom. "There's still more screws to sort," he said. "You come by next week and finish." Then he walked off.

Boom fought the urge to kick his legs forward and back. He didn't want to trip up one of the passing men, but sitting still was the worst kind of torture. Forget about stretching someone on the rack, or shoving splinters under someone's fingernails. Just sit two kids on a bench and tell them not to move.

Finally the cars stopped coming and the double doors to the hall shut, leaving Boom and Winger and the baby alone in the entryway. Drumming echoed from deep beyond the doors. Men's voices rose in song.

Sons of the Vikings
Are we, are we.
Ancestors mighty
They be, they be.
Though they're dead and gone
Their blood will still flow on.

Sons of the Vikings are we.
ARE WE!

Added to the drumming and singing came a great deal of stomping. Boom squirmed with curiosity. What had Halvor meant *exactly* when he'd told them not to move? Obviously Boom had to move in order to breathe. He had to move his eyelids or his eyeballs would dry out. Halvor couldn't have literally meant "don't move." People should be precise when giving instructions. If lungs and eyelids could move, then feet should be able to move as well, taking the entire body with them. Boom tiptoed forward, followed by Winger.

The boys knelt outside the great oak doors, taking turns at the keyhole. Boom could get only a narrow view of men's legs. The guy in the fuzzy slippers marched by. Boom found himself humming along to the song, recognizing it as the same tune that Halvor often hummed while cooking. A horn blew and Winger nearly jumped out of his socks. The baby whimpered. The drumming and marching ceased.

"Vikings, be seated!" someone yelled. "Attend to roll call." Each man answered as his name was called. "Where's Maurice the Menace?"

"Maurice's wife wouldn't let him come tonight. His mother-in-law is visiting."

"Very well. Who has called the emergency meeting?"

"I did." Though Boom could not see the speaker, he immediately knew the voice.

"Then take the sacred staff and speak, Halvor the Humble."

Halvor the Humble? *Strange choice,* Boom thought. He should have chosen Halvor the Hacker of Fish, or Halvor the Huge.

Boom's legs started to ache from crouching, but he continued to press his eye to the keyhole. He couldn't get a glimpse of the front of the hall, and now that the men were seated, all he could see was the backs of their heads.

"My turn," Winger whispered, impatiently elbowing Boom.

"I ask each and every one of you to swear an oath of secrecy, for sure," Halvor told the men. "What I'm about to tell you must never leave this room."

"By the blood of Thor, we swear an oath of secrecy," the men chanted.

"Then I shall just come right out and say it." Boom's pulse beat rapidly at the side of his neck. "Boom, the boy I care for, has found a merbaby."

Boom expected a round of gasps to fill the hall. Instead, what echoed off the walls was laughter, quickly turning to mumbles of irritation.

"You called me from Edith's meat loaf for this?"

"What kind of game are you playing?"

"You've always been a crazy one, Halvor. Haven't I always said that Halvor was a crazy one?"

"You are beholden to hear me out, for I hold the sacred staff," Halvor bellowed. That seemed to get their attention, and the voices quieted. Halvor cleared his throat. "Boom brought the creature home, ignorant of its horrible powers, ignorant of the curse that sickens anyone who takes a mermaid's child. The curse has fallen on Mertyle, the girl I care for. Just like Erik the Red's firstborn daughter, Mertyle's life is in jeopardy. Only the baby's mother can lift the curse." More mumbling. "I speak the truth. May the wrath of Thor be upon me if I don't. Mertyle needs our help and she needs it now!"

"How can we believe you, Halvor?" a man asked. "We've heard the stories of Erik the Red's firstborn daughter, but no one here has ever seen a mermaid."

"Once again I ask you to swear the oath."

"By the blood of Thor, we swear the oath of secrecy."

"Open the doors," Halvor called. The double doors opened, sending Boom and Winger scrambling to their feet. "Bring in the baby."

This could be a huge mistake, Boom thought as he and Winger each took a handle and carried the laundry basket into the hall. The stuffed heads of bison, elk, and moose stared from the cedar wall with their glass eyes. An aisle stretched down the center of the room, flanked on either side by men in Viking helmets and animal pelts who sat on wooden benches. At the front stood a long table made from a tree that had been split lengthwise. A fire burned in a massive riverstone hearth, its flame dancing madly as wind furled down the chimney. The hall smelled like a damp forest.

The basket shook, as did Boom's and Winger's hands.

Boom felt like the Cowardly Lion, approaching the Great Wizard of Oz. He wanted to tuck his tail between his legs and run.

He and Winger placed the basket on the long table. "Show them," Halvor said. Boom hesitated, turning to look at the furrowed faces, at the beards and ruddy cheeks, at the bushy eyebrows and tousled manes of hair. Except for the fuzzy slippers and the crocheted scarves, this was how the Vikings themselves must have looked. What would these men do when they saw the merbaby? Was he dooming her to a horrible end? His trembling hands rested on the blanket.

"It will be okay, Boom," Halvor whispered in his ear. "Show them."

"Show us, show us," the men chanted.

This was like showing a bunny to a pack of hungry wolves. Well, a ferocious, nasty little mutant bunny.

Boom pulled off the blanket. The merbaby sprang up on her tail and bared her teeth — a formidable striking position that, even though he'd seen it many times, still scared the pants off Boom. A roar rose in the throats of the Viking descendants, and they reached under the benches and grabbed spears and axes and pointed them at the baby.

"No!" Boom cried, stepping in front of the table. "You can't hurt it. Mertyle made me promise that no one would hurt it."

"It's a sworn enemy," a man cried, waving a drumstick and a spear.

"It's just a baby," Boom argued. The men quieted a bit. "It's just a baby and Mertyle loves it."

It is well known that the blood of a direct Viking descendant carries the traditions of the ancient world. A Viking descendant understands the importance of pickling fish so that there will be food in times of famine. A Viking descendant knows which trees will make the best ships. A Viking descendant understands the unforgiving nature of storms at sea, the thirst for revenge, and the desire for exploration.

But what most outsiders do not realize is that the blood of a direct Viking descendant carries the passions of the ancient world as well, and the passion that Viking descendants best understand is love. Lives were so short-lived in those dark days, and heartache so common, that the Vikings wrote the most beautiful love poems to ever come from the human heart. And that poetry coursed like a raging river through the blood of the men who stood in the great cedar hall.

"Love," they repeated, lowering their weapons. The creased faces softened, the fire in their eyes dampened. "Love," they whispered to each other.

Halvor tapped the staff on the floor. "Mertyle's very sick. The doctor's never seen her illness because it's not of the human world. It's the merfolk's curse, as clear as day. We've got to get this baby back to its mother so the curse will be lifted."

Boom reached into his jacket pocket and pulled out the

paper from the print shop. "I think this is a map," he said, holding it out. "A map of the merfolk."

The fishing boat captain stepped forward. It took Boom a moment to recognize him, since he wore a horned helmet and a badger-skin cape. The captain eyed the baby, who was still in striking position. "That be the reject fish?" he asked. Boom nodded. "Then I am responsible for this situation. I must help you the best I can." He slid a pair of reading glasses up his nose and took the map from Boom's hand. "Sure, it be a map. There's the horizon." He pointed to the line in the center of the drawing. "The night sky above and the ocean below."

Just as Boom thought. "It's an island, isn't it?" he asked excitedly.

"Very good, lad. It be an island and I know which one it be. Whale Fin Island."

Boom had thought that the shape looked like a witch's hat, but a whale fin seemed a good description as well.

Halvor scratched his beard. "Where in Thor's name is Whale Fin Island?"

The captain took off his glasses. "Whale Fin Island be about a day's sail from Fairweather and not far from Pelican Beak Island, where I caught the wee creature. It be a lonely little island. No one lives there but the seals and gulls."

"We must leave immediately," Halvor urged. "You must take us there."

To Boom's surprise, the captain shook his head. "Me boat's too old to take the storm," he said. "Even with a strong boat, I wouldn't recommend setting sail in such a wind. The wind will blow you right off course. Wait until it passes."

"But we can't wait," Boom cried. They had to understand. "Mertyle might die. She might not see the year's end — might not even see tomorrow."

"Then you'll have to get yourself a boat," the captain said. "I'd be happy to skipper it, but I don't know anyone willing to risk their boat in such a storm."

Boom searched the faces until his gaze rested on Mr. Jorgenson. "Can we use your boat?" he asked. The retired police chief raised his eyebrows.

"My boat? My Viking ship?"

"Yes," Boom said. "What ship could better save a little girl's life than a Viking ship? Unless . . ."

"Unless what?" Mr. Jorgenson asked suspiciously.

"Unless you don't think your ship can take a storm." Boom folded his arms. Would he take the bait?

Silence filled the hall as everyone waited for Mr. Jorgenson to respond. As he stepped forward, cedar shavings fell from his pant legs. "A Viking ship can take any storm. You've got yourself a boat."

Chapter Twenty-six:

FAME and FORTUNE

Nothing could be accomplished in the dark of night. After much discussion it was decided that the captain, whose name was Igor, and Mr. Jorgenson, who had carved the ship, and a fellow named Burt, who had won the Viking tree-tossing contest, would accompany Halvor, Boom, Winger, Mertyle, and the merbaby on the journey. That was as many people as the boat could safely carry. Captain Igor went off to fetch his charts while Mr. Jorgenson went to hook up his boat trailer to his truck. Burt went to tell his wife that he'd be gone at sea for a few days. The rest of the Viking membership filed out of the cedar hall, each aglow with a new sense of wonder and pride in their heritage.

"If the merfolk are real, does this mean those stories about the two-headed serpents are real?" fuzzy-slipper man asked on his way out.

"Guess so," another man answered.

"Come, boys. Let's go home and prepare," Halvor said.

It was already morning, though it was hard to tell through the heavy clouds that encircled Fairweather Island. The storm let loose, churning up the sea, overturning garbage cans, and filling the gutters with rain. Back at the Brooms', the nervous crew prepared for their journey.

"Dress for bad weather," Halvor advised, donning a wool cap and a heavy peacoat. Mertyle, weakened and dizzy, needed help with her layers. Boom tugged and buttoned as his sister complained that she was too hot. With her white, fuzzy face sandwiched between a black knit hat and a black turtleneck sweater, she looked like an Oreo. No one bothered to layer the baby. After all, she swam in icy ocean water, so a drop in the temperature wouldn't bother her. She lay in the laundry basket, snoring like a dog with a head cold.

Winger called his mom again. She'd find out if he missed school, so he had to tell her a partial truth. She basically freaked out. "A Viking ship?" Everyone could hear her voice screeching through the receiver. "A Viking ship? You'll drown! You go to school, young man, so you can win that certificate." Winger always had perfect attendance, which always earned him a certificate for a month's supply of ice cream sundaes at the Fairweather Dairy Emporium and a notice in the *Fairweather News,* which Mrs. Wingingham liked to show her friends. "You go to school."

He hung up the phone. "I'm sorry. I can't go," he said to Boom. "But you know I'd do anything for Mertyle." His cheeks turned red the way they always did when he said Mertyle's name.

"I know," Boom told him. "When you get to school, tell Principal Prunewallop that Mertyle and I have the swine flu. That way she won't make me do detention in her office."

"Okay," Winger agreed.

"Button up, everyone," Halvor said. "It's cold outside."

"I don't want to go," Mertyle whimpered. "I can't leave."

"You have to go," Winger told her. "You have to get better, Mertyle." He gave her a hug. With a lingering look, and after spitting out a stray fuzzy, he left for school.

Mr. Broom, who had spent the night in the entryway closet, came out for a moment to eat some rye toast, but the sound of the wind raging down the chimney sent him fleeing back to his safe cave. So caught up in his own world, he didn't notice that his daughter's appearance had changed dramatically, nor did he notice that everyone was dressed for a sea journey.

It would have taken Boom too much time to explain the situation to his father anyway. "We'll just have to leave him a note," he decided. "I'll write that we'll be back in a few days." Boom couldn't bring himself to tell his father that Mertyle might die. He was afraid the truth would send his father to a place that was deeper and darker than the closet.

Boom zipped up his jacket just as Winger rushed back inside, waving a newspaper. "Big trouble," he cried, his glasses fogging. "Big, big, big trouble!" He pressed the paper into Boom's face. Boom stepped back so he could actually see the front page.

BOY FINDS MERBABY, the headline read. Beneath the headline was a black-and-white photo of Boom holding the baby as he crouched behind the garbage cans in the Mumps' yard.

"Big trouble," Winger repeated, raindrops dripping from his nose.

Boom took a deep breath and read aloud as the others gathered.

> A security camera snapped this photo on the property of Mr. Theodore Mump of 1 Prosperity Street. The photo shows a boy, identified as Boom Broom of 0 Prosperity Street, holding what seems to be an actual merbaby.
>
> "It's true," Mr. Mump's son, Hurley, told this reporter. "I held it and it's green and it's real. And it belongs to me. I found it. Boom stole it."
>
> "Boom Broom is a thief and he was trespassing," Mr. Mump said.
>
> If Hurley Mump found a merbaby, it can only be described as the discovery of the twenty-first century. The Broom household could not be contacted for a response, but this reporter is determined to get to the truth of this amazing story. More to follow in tomorrow's edition.

"A thief?" Boom cried. How dare those Mumps call him a thief!

The phone rang. "Hello?" Halvor said. He listened and then shook his head angrily. "We have no comment." He hung up the phone but a moment later it rang again. He unplugged the cord with a curse. "May the wrath of Thor be upon those Mumps," he bellowed.

The wrath of Thor would be good, if Thor's wrath meant that the Mumps would be squeezed and popped like the bloodsucking fleas that they were. Boom crumpled the paper and threw it on the floor, kicking it down the hall. He had wanted to be famous for his discovery, but not like this. He had dreamt of riches, but not with so much at stake. Fame and fortune meant nothing to him now. They were empty jars with no dandelions, if Mertyle didn't make it.

"We can't let Hurley call Boom a thief!" Winger exclaimed.

"We don't have any more time to think about the Mumps," Halvor told his visibly upset crew. "We'll need a bit of food for the journey." He tucked some marmalade and bread into a duffel bag, along with a few cans of salmon and a can opener. He poured an ample supply of cat food and water into Fluffy's bowls.

Boom ran upstairs and fed the remaining goldfish, then ran back downstairs. "Let's go."

"Outside," Mertyle mumbled, chewing on her fingernails. Aside from her eyeballs, Mertyle's fingernails appeared to be the only other part of her not covered with fuzz. "Will you leave a note for Mom, too? Just in case?"

Boom nodded and pretended to scribble a few more lines on the note he had written for his father. Whatever it took to get Mertyle to leave the house.

Halvor swung the duffel bag over his shoulder. "Okay, everyone, let's go find the merfolk, for sure."

Boom covered the baby with the blanket and picked up the laundry basket. Halvor opened the front door, and Boom stepped outside to the explosive sound of camera shutters. A dozen microphones were shoved in his face.

"What can you tell us about the merbaby?"

"We'll pay you two thousand dollars for an exclusive interview."

"Don't listen to him. We'll pay you three thousand."

Boom couldn't breathe with so many faces staring down at him. They crowded on the sagging porch, pushing one another to get their microphones closer to Boom. Photographers held cameras above their heads and madly snapped. Flashbulbs popped and sizzled. Reporters threw so many questions Boom's way, he felt like a wall and the questions were the red rubber balls hitting him square on, one right after the other. He froze with a grimace.

"Boom, where are you going with that laundry basket?"

"Boom, where are you hiding the baby?"

"Do you intend to harm the creature?"

"Did you steal it from Hurley Mump?"

Halvor pulled Boom back into the house and closed the door. "We're surrounded by sharks," he snarled, dropping the duffel bag and grabbing his axe. "We'll have to hack our way out of here, for sure."

"No," Boom said, fearful that Halvor might be serious.

Mertyle began to cry. "I'm so itchy."

Halvor looked at his watch. "It's already 8 a.m. Mr. Jorgenson, Captain Igor, and Burt will be waiting for us."

"How are we going to get out of here?" Winger asked.

Boom pulled back the curtain in the entryway window and peered out at the madness. Dozens of vans with satellite dishes had parked in the street. Reporters and camera crews dashed up and down the walkway, fighting the wind and rain. The dirt circle had turned into a mud bog, and one lady slipped and sprayed mud all over some of her colleagues. Mr. Mump started waving to everyone from his driveway. "Over here," he yelled. "I'll tell you all about the merbaby." The reporters dashed across the street. Mr. Mump opened his garage door and Mrs. Mump started handing out cream-filled cupcakes and finger sandwiches. Hurley Mump appeared, his hair slicked back, dressed in his Sunday suit even though it was Monday morning. He smiled as reporters jammed their microphones at him. This was the morning that Boom had planned to demand a rematch. The rematch now seemed as insignificant as Hurley's smirk.

"I wish they'd all go away," Mertyle said.

Of course!

"Mertyle, tell that to the baby. Make another wish." Boom shook his sister's drooping shoulders. "Make the wish. Hurry." He lifted the blanket but the basket was empty. He looked around. "Where is it?"

"There," Winger cried. The baby had flopped her way to the top of the stairs, heading for the bedroom.

Boom didn't need anyone to convince him to go get the creature. Regardless of how much spitting and growling she did, this was not the time for cowardice. He ran up the stairs and found the baby chewing on his slippers. "You've got to let me pick you up again," he told her, reaching forward. She greeted Boom in her usual manner. Boom wiped the spray of spit from his cheeks as the baby snarled and thumped her tail on the carpet. She wasn't going to make this easy. She might even draw blood again. She didn't seem to care that Mertyle was growing sicker by the minute. At that moment, Boom felt all the sadness he had been holding in for the entire year come percolating to the surface.

"Please, Baby. Please let me take you. You're the only chance Mertyle has. She's got to get better. I can't lose her, too." Though he fought hard to hold them back, tears pooled in his lower lids. A single tear overflowed onto his cheek and dripped onto the carpet as he wiped the others away. The baby leaned forward and touched the fallen tear, turning it into a crystal. She picked it up and held it out to Boom.

"Thank you," he said, accepting the amazing gift.

The merbaby held out her arms and Boom picked her

up. He stared into the depths of her eyes where her iris danced like ships on the sea. "You are the most amazing discovery of the twenty-first century. Of any century."

"Boom!" Halvor hollered from downstairs.

Boom carried the baby to the window and pointed to the chaos in progress outside. "Can you get rid of all those people? For Mertyle's sake?"

The baby stuck her hand in Boom's jacket pocket and pulled out one of the three dollar bills. She looked at the money, then at Boom, then out the window. She pointed as a delivery van pulled in between two television station trucks. Neither the Mumps nor the reporters took notice. They were too busy with Hurley and the cupcakes, too busy keeping themselves dry from the rain and safe from the wind.

The delivery guy got out and opened the back of his van, pulling out boxes labeled DEPARTMENT OF TREASURY.

Chapter Twenty-seven:

MR. BROOM EMERGES

Winger," Boom cried, rushing down the stairs with the baby in his arms. "Go outside and open those boxes. They're full of money."

"Money?" Winger pulled back the curtain.

"Start giving it away."

"Give it away? Boom, are you crazy? There's, like, twenty boxes out there."

It did sound crazy, but money wouldn't cure Mertyle. "It's a distraction," Boom explained. "To help Mertyle."

"Oh. Okay, then." Winger opened the door. "Good luck,

everyone." He scurried around the mud circle and ran toward the van, yelling, "Hey, look over here! FREE MONEY!"

The reaction was exactly what Boom had hoped for. The reporters dropped their microphones and the camera crews dropped their equipment as Winger held up fists full of dollars. The wind claimed some of the bills, scattering them across the street. Like hungry raccoons fighting over ripe bananas, the reporters pushed and shoved and fought to grab as much money as possible. The Mumps, with their stout bodies and greedy dispositions, fought their way into the center of the crowd.

"The coast is clear," Boom said.

Out the back door went Halvor, Mertyle, Boom, and the baby. Across the edge of the yard they hurried, over the fence, and into the trampled cornfield. No one on Prosperity Street took notice. The scent of money polluted the air and filled every nostril. The money-grabbers screamed and kicked one another, stuffing the bills into pockets and down shirts.

Halvor took Mertyle's arm as they ran across the field, helping her keep her balance. Boom had tucked the baby in his jacket. Her green face peeked out like a pea in a pod. They came to the edge of the forest and Boom looked over his shoulder, relieved to see that no one was following. The baby clung tightly to Boom as they ran down a path strewn with fallen branches. Through the windswept trees they hurried until they came to the cliff's edge. Mr. Jorgenson's boat floated in the sloppy sea below. The sight of the majestic ship, with its dragon figurehead and graceful keel, would have made the real Vikings proud. Captain Igor waved from the steering oar.

Down the steep trail they stumbled, slowing at each of the switchbacks until they reached the water. The tide swelled high and the sea slapped against the cliff's face. Mr. Jorgenson rowed up in his rowboat. "Bless your heart, Mertyle," he said when he looked upon her fuzzy face. As Mertyle climbed in, he yelled above the wind's howl. "Burt couldn't come. His wife said he had to stay home and unclog the bathroom sink."

"Down two men," Halvor grumbled. "Winger and Burt. That's not good. In this storm we need all the rowing hands we can get."

"You're right, but where can we get another pair of hands?" Mr. Jorgenson asked.

Boom looked back up the cliff. He'd climbed the trail many times in his life but had never run it. He handed the baby to Mertyle. "I'll go get another pair of hands," he said. "I'll be back as soon as I can."

His heart pounded as he forced his limbs up the steep path. He didn't stop to rest, not once, as he ran through the forest and across the cornfield. The wind continued its crazy dance, whistling in his ears and snaking around his face. Would Hurley help them? Mr. Mump seemed strong, but would he care enough to help his neighbors?

Mr. Mump had backed his truck next to the delivery van and was fighting over the boxes. Hurley and Daisy stood in the truck's bed, kicking people as they tried to climb in to get their hands on more money. Everyone was screaming at everyone else.

Forget them, Boom thought. *I know who will help.*

Boom ran through his back door, right to the hall closet. "Dad?" he called, opening the door.

Mr. Broom's long hair hung in his face, matted with nervous sweat. He clung to a mop. "The twister. Has it come again?" he asked. "Is that why everyone is screaming?"

"No, Dad. There's no twister." Boom knelt inside the closet and took his dad's trembling hands. "Dad, we need your help. You must listen to me. Mertyle's in danger."

"Mertyle?" Mr. Broom's hands stopped shaking and he looked directly into Boom's eyes. "My little Mertyle?"

"She's sick for real this time and we're trying to get her to the people who can cure her. We have to row to Whale Fin Island and we need your help."

"Where is she?"

"Outside. She's outside. We have to go outside, Dad."

Mr. Broom gasped. "Out of the house? Into the wind?"

"Yes, Dad, into the wind. Mom's not here to help us. You've got to be the one."

"Into the wind?"

Boom lost all patience. "Mertyle might die!" he yelled. Boom was the child and the quivering mass on the floor was supposed to be the adult. "Get up and help us," Boom begged. "Please, Dad. Don't you see that if I can go outside, then so can you? Don't you think I was scared after Mom died? I wanted to crawl under my bed but I didn't. I went outside, and you can do it too." He took a deep, frenzied breath. "We can't let Mertyle die. I don't want Mertyle to die. She needs us."

Mr. Broom's eyes widened. "Die? My little Mertyle?" He put down the mop, and the dazed mask that he had worn for the past year seemed to melt away. "Then I must go," he said, crawling out of the closet. Boom helped him to his feet and handed him a coat. Mr. Broom put it on with trembling hands. "I must go *outside*." Mr. Broom took a cautious step out the back door, wincing as the wind whipped his face. "Outside," he repeated. Boom took his father's hand and pulled him free of the house that had become his prison.

Mr. Broom was a good runner and he kept pace with Boom as they crossed the cornfield. "See, Dad," Boom yelled, pumping his legs. "The wind won't hurt us. There's nothing to be worried about."

"No twisters?" Mr. Broom asked.

"No twisters," Boom told him.

Had Boom hesitated before answering, he would not have said what he said. Because a mere two seconds later, a sound approached, similar to the sound Halvor's blender made when chopping fish fins. Boom looked over his shoulder, expecting to see a reporter's helicopter. But the sky above his house had turned black and a thick cloud swirled above it, churning and tossing rainbow dandelions every which way.

A twister! In the name of Thor, a twister!

Both Boom and Mr. Broom screamed so loud that Boom thought they might burst their lungs. The Mumps and the reporters began to scream as well. Fear seized hold of Boom's body but he knew there was no time for fear. He pulled his dad's arm until they reached the forest's edge. They turned to check the twister's progress. The Broom house still stood, but the churning spiral of wind kicked up bits of cornstalk as it raced across the field. Into the forest Boom and his father ran as the twister followed, tearing out saplings as if they were mere fish kebob skewers.

"Run!" Boom screamed, as the twister came closer.

They stopped at the cliff's edge. Below, the others waved from the Viking ship, then screamed and pointed as the twister appeared at the top of the cliff. Down the trail father and son ran. Mr. Broom lost his balance, sliding to the first switchback. Boom slipped as well, but regained his footing. Rocks tumbled by as the twister touched the cliff's edge. They weren't going to make it. No way. The twister would overtake them.

The tide had risen higher and the Viking ship drifted close to the cliff's face. "Jump!" Captain Igor shouted.

"Jump!" echoed Halvor.

Jump? Were they nuts?

A rock hit Mr. Broom in the shoulder, and Boom turned to see the edge of the twister within reach. The force of it stung his entire body. He grabbed his father's hand, and together they jumped.

Chapter Twenty-eight

MAN OVERBOARD

Boom's face was pressed against someone's coat. He sat up and wiped drool from his chin. He was lying on the deck of Mr. Jorgenson's ship. He must have passed out, or maybe he had hit his head on something. His back ached, as did his legs — the sure result of having jumped off a cliff.

The jump was the last thing he remembered. Just how long had he been knocked out? Mertyle lay next to him, snoring. The white fuzz had grown through her black sweater and pants and had so thoroughly transformed her that, had she not been wearing tennis shoes, Boom might have thought the abominable snowman had come for a visit. Which would be completely believable at this point in his life.

Boom peered over the ship's rail. Where were they exactly? The cliffs of Fairweather Island could not be seen, nor any land, for that matter. He remembered that the twister had been hot on his heels. Was it possible that the raging wind had carried the ship somewhere, just as it had carried his mother?

The twister was gone, the rain had stopped, and the rays from the low winter sun fell like yellow ribbons across the calm sea. Boom turned to look for the others and found Captain Igor, Mr. Jorgenson, Halvor, and Mr. Broom strewn about the deck like fish out of water — limp and gasping for air. Had they all hit their heads from the force of the twister? Had it knocked the breath out of everyone? The sky showed no signs of the morning's storm. In fact, there was no wind whatsoever. Not a breeze, not a whisper, not even a sigh. A dandelion seed ball could have lounged on deck without worry of being blown overboard.

The sea lapped at the sides of the boat as gently as a cat at its milk bowl. One could call it the calm after the storm, but only if referring to the weather — for a storm still raged inside of Boom. A storm of worry and anger. Worry for his sister's life and anger at the universe for playing with his family as if they were nothing more than brine shrimp in a classroom beaker. Another twister, indeed!

Boom was about to check on his sister when a flash of blue-green darted past the boat.

The merbaby!

"Hey!" he yelled as the baby arched her tail and dove below the water's surface. "Hey! What are you doing?" Boom's heart began to race. Was the creature going to swim away? Would she leave them behind and find her mother on her own? If so, there would be no one to remove Mertyle's curse. "You get back here right now!"

The baby didn't pay any attention to Boom. She swam under the boat.

"What's all the hollering?" Halvor complained, rubbing his head.

"The merbaby," Boom said, running to the other side of the boat. "It's in the water!"

Everyone, except Mertyle, woke with a start and ran to the rail. There was no time for grogginess or yawning, no time for "Where are we?" or "Does anyone know how I got this bump on my noggin?" The merbaby was getting away.

While Mr. Jorgenson's ship was a perfect replica of a Viking ship, from the curved prow to the square sail, it was, to be exact, one-eighth the size. So when everyone ran to look at the baby, the boat heeled.

"There it is!" Boom cried, pointing at the little green head that poked up for a breath of air. The baby squirted some water from her mouth and dove under the boat again. "There it goes." Boom ran to the port side. The others followed, tipping the boat as they went.

"She be starboard again," Captain Igor yelled, and back they ran. "Now she be port side." Halvor and Mr. Jorgenson had to stop to catch their breath. They held their hands over their equally rotund stomachs as they gasped.

"That's a very bad fishy," Halvor grumbled.

Mr. Jorgenson's eyeballs rolled back and he moaned. "I don't feel so good. Every one stop rocking the boat." But Boom wasn't about to stop rocking the boat. He couldn't let that baby out of his sight. Back to starboard he and Captain Igor ran.

Mr. Broom, however, knelt over Mertyle, softly calling her name. "Oh, my little Mertyle. What has happened to you?" He hugged her. "She's awake," he told the others. "But she can't speak. Her mouth is all fuzzy."

There had once been a time, many times in fact, when Boom had wished that his sister couldn't speak. When she had gone on and on about facts learned on *Jeopardy!* or on and on about something she had seen with the magnifying glass. But at that moment, not being able to speak seemed a very bad thing because no one could know how Mertyle felt. No one could know if the mermaid's curse was nearing the end — Mertyle's end. Boom ran back to the port side as the baby dove again.

"Get a net," Captain Igor ordered. "That be how I caught the wee rascal in the first place."

"Yah, good idea," Halvor said. "Where's your net, Jorgenson?"

Mr. Jorgenson opened a crate and pulled out a rolled-up fishing net. He took one end and began unraveling, while Halvor took the other end.

Captain Igor slid a small telescope from his pocket and stood next to Boom. "There she be," he said, peering through the scope as the baby splashed in the distance. "We'll have to coax her in a bit closer. Bring the net, lads."

Halvor and Mr. Jorgenson seemed to be having a bit of trouble with the net. They pushed and pulled like a game of tug-of-war. "You're tangling it, for sure," Halvor complained.

"Don't tell me *I'm* tangling it. *I'm* a direct descendant of Ned the Net-maker and I know how to work a net." Mr. Jorgenson's arms were buried deep in the twisted mass of cord. "You're the one tangling it."

"I'm not the one tangling it," Halvor bellowed. "I'm a direct descendant of Fritz the Fisherman and net-working's in my blood, for sure." They glared at each other, puffing out their chests like feisty puffer-fish.

"Stop doing that. You're making it worse." The net was now wrapped around Mr. Jorgenson's waist.

"*I'm* making it worse?" Halvor's legs became so entwined that he fell over and landed on his bottom with a big thud. Mr. Jorgenson fell as well. The two started struggling like reject seafood.

"That be a sorry sight," Captain Igor said, shaking his head as the Viking descendants wound themselves up so tightly that they could no longer move. But Boom had something more important on his mind — that darn baby. She continued her playful behavior, frolicking from port to starboard, stopping every so often to cast a devilish look Boom's way.

"Baby," Boom called out. "Please come back." She seemed to be enjoying herself as she spun on her tail and somersaulted. If she swam away or got eaten by a shark, all would be lost. Mertyle would be lost. There was only one thing to do. Boom took off his coat and pulled off his black sneakers and socks.

"She be changing course again," Captain Igor said, adjusting the scope.

Boom stripped down to his underpants and undershirt, each equally full of holes and in need of a good washing. He looked over at Mertyle, who lay with her head resting against Mr. Broom's chest. Father and son stared into each other's eyes. For the first time, Boom felt that his own eyes held as much fear as his father's did. Then he turned and dove into the sea.

"Boom! No!" Mr. Broom cried out.

"Man overboard!" the captain yelled.

It wasn't a graceful dive — half belly flop, half sprawl. Boom held his breath as the cold slapped him hard. How could the merbaby stand to swim in such icy water? Fish are cold-blooded, but humans are warm-blooded. She had to be mostly made of fish to endure such temperatures. He lifted his face for air and found himself looking straight at the merbaby. He wanted to yell at her, to tell her that she was a bad baby for leaving the boat, but yelling might scare her away.

Boom knew he wouldn't be able to take the cold much longer. He began to tread water, which he did quite well thanks to the advantage of his big foot. "Please come back to the boat," he begged. The baby did a somersault and began swimming circles around him.

"Boom!" Mr. Broom yelled, starting to climb over the rail. The baby stopped swimming and growled.

"No, Dad. You can't come in. You'll scare off the baby." But Mr. Broom kept climbing. "Dad, I'm fine. You've got to let me do this. For Mertyle's sake." Mr. Broom paused, then reluctantly climbed back on deck. "I'm fine!" Boom assured him.

But Boom wasn't completely fine. An eerie thought came over him and his heart started to race. The merfolk had pulled Erik the Red's wife from Erik's ship and drowned her. Boom curled his toes, imagining hands reaching up from the murky depths to clutch his ankles. The cold pierced through to his bones, making his legs ache. He reached out and tried to grab the baby, but she smacked his hand with her tail.

"Boom!" Mr. Broom called. "Grab this." A flotation ring landed with a splash nearby.

"Baby," Boom said with a shivering jaw. "Mertyle needs you to come back to the boat."

The baby shook her head and pointed. Boom turned and realized why the baby would not come back. At the bow of Mr. Jorgenson's replica ship, on top of a crate, sat a Viking helmet. A shiny Viking helmet that reflected the sun's rays like a beacon.

"Captain Igor," Boom yelled, clinging to the flotation ring. "Get rid of that helmet. It scares the baby."

Mr. Jorgenson, though still entwined in the netting, managed to pop his head over the rail. "That helmet was worn by Englebert the Explorer in the fifth century A.D. That helmet is priceless."

"Vikings didn't wear horned helmets," Boom cried, remembering Mertyle's words. "It's not a real artifact."

"What nonsense," Mr. Jorgenson said. "Everyone knows that Vikings wore horned helmets."

"Yah, for sure," chimed Halvor.

Captain Igor rushed to the bow and picked up the helmet. "It says 'Made in China.'"

"Get rid of it," Boom pleaded, desperate to get out of the cold. His head felt as if it were being squeezed in a vise, and he couldn't feel his lower half at all. Captain Igor tossed the helmet into the sea as Mr. Jorgenson screamed like a girl.

"My helmet! Eeeeeeehhhhhhhh!"

Boom wiped seaweed from his face. "Now will you come back to the boat?" The baby grabbed the flotation ring and nodded. Like a speedboat, she propelled them back to the Viking ship.

Chapter Twenty-nine

The CALM AFTER the STORM

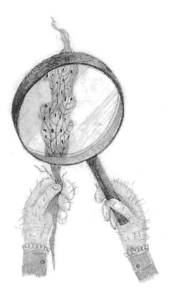

With the merbaby back on board, and Halvor and Mr. Jorgenson untangled, all eyes turned to Mertyle. The fuzz, once growing straight up in the air like Boom's hair, had gone limp. That couldn't be a good sign. "We've got to hurry up and find the baby's mother," Boom said, pulling his clothing back on.

"How do we do that?" Mr. Broom asked. Who could blame him for his confusion? He had been living in the closet during most of the weekend, and though everyone had tried to bring him up to speed, he had a lot of information to absorb. He would later tell his children that it was like waking up from a trance or a bout of amnesia. "What island are we sailing to?"

"Whale Fin Island," Captain Igor said, opening his telescope and scanning the horizon. "That twister could have dropped us anywhere." He unrolled a chart and spread it on the deck. Then he placed the map from the print shop next to it. "Whale Fin Island be dead north of Fairweather, but since I don't know exactly where the twister dropped us, I can't be certain how far or in which direction we have to go."

No one else seemed to know either. Halvor scratched his beard and Mr. Jorgenson mumbled something about his priceless helmet. Boom felt completely helpless. He didn't know doodley-squat about navigation.

Suddenly, Mertyle moved. All eyes turned to her again. Very slowly, she reached out her fuzzy arm, waving the magnifying glass. Boom leaned close. "What is it, Mertyle?" He pushed the fuzz away so he could look into her eyes. She was still in there, trapped behind the furry mask. She reached out her other arm and pulled a piece of seaweed from Boom's hair. Then she put the magnifying glass over the seaweed.

Now was not the time to be examining things. What was the matter with her, besides the obvious? What could she possibly be thinking?

"Poor Mertyle," Halvor whispered. "She's confused."

Mr. Broom wrapped his arms around Mertyle. The baby glared at them from across the deck with an expression that was unmistakable jealousy. Fish do have feelings, Boom realized.

Again, Mertyle put the glass over the seaweed.

"She loves that glass as much as her mother did," Mr. Broom said sadly. "Milly carried it everywhere."

"Milly Broom could solve any mystery the department sent her way," Mr. Jorgenson recalled. "When I was chief of police, I relied on her all the time. She saw things through that glass that no one else could see."

"Mertyle's a direct descendant of Mrs. Broom, for sure," Halvor said.

Mertyle kept waving the glass. "I think she's trying to tell us something," Boom realized. He took the glass and seaweed. *She saw things no one else could see.* Like the map, for instance. Mertyle had been right about that drawing on the merbaby's scale. Boom's thoughts raced ahead, trying to figure out why his sister would want to examine a piece of seaweed. He put the seaweed on the deck and looked through the glass.

"It just looks like a piece of spinach," he said, as the others huddled around. "It's green." Mertyle nudged Boom with her foot. Then she nudged him again. He looked back through the lens, harder this time, looking for something that no one else saw. Going beyond the surface of the plant — beyond the obvious. He squinted, staring into the green depths. And there, next to an array of green veins, tiny red dots shimmered. "It has red dots," Boom announced.

"Red dots?" Captain Igor asked. "Let me see that." He took the magnifying glass and peered at the blob of greenery. "Why, this be Northern Leopard Seaweed. It only grows in the waters off Salt Rim Island." Captain Igor stood. "That means that the twister has dropped us north of Whale Fin Island. We have to backtrack, lads. We have to go south." He licked his finger and held it up. "Not a touch of wind. We'll have to row."

"Wait," Boom said as the men went to grab oars. "Mermaids can grant wishes."

"Oh?" Captain Igor asked. "I never knew that."

Boom crouched next to the baby. "I know you have something against granting *my* wishes," he said, "but this time it's really important. If we can find your mother, then you can go home and Mertyle can get well." The baby picked some kelp from her belly button. Boom closed his eyes and crossed his fingers. "I wish we could be at Whale Fin Island."

Upon opening his eyes, it did not surprise him to see that nothing had happened. The baby stuck the piece of kelp up her nose, not at all taking the situation seriously.

"We know that the baby can't lift the curse," Halvor reminded Boom. "Maybe she can't help us at all."

"Or maybe it just doesn't care," Boom said through clenched teeth, making sure he spoke loud enough for the baby to hear.

"Looks like we've got some rowing ahead of us," Captain Igor said.

The captain took his place at the steering oar. Mr. Broom and Boom sat on the port side of the boat, Halvor and Mr. Jorgenson sat on the starboard side. As soon as Mr. Broom left Mertyle, the baby flopped over and sat in her lap. Like sitting on a polar-bear-skin rug.

The task at hand was to get to Whale Fin Island as quickly as possible. Boom had never rowed before. He wrapped his hands over the wooden oar but didn't quite know what to do.

"In my day," Mr. Jorgenson declared, gripping his oar, "we rowed every morning for exercise, no matter what the weather. None of those fancy gyms in my day. We rowed until our hands bled. Then we walked all the way to school."

While the other oarsmen pulled their oars through the water, Boom's skimmed the surface. His hands slipped and he fell backward. "Darn it!" he cried. He sat back on the bench and tried again. If he moved the oar faster, then they'd get there faster, but the faster he tried to move it, the more it slipped from his grip.

"Steady there, lad," Captain Igor called.

The story of firstborn Mertyle echoed in Boom's mind. She hadn't lived to see the year's end. "We have to get there!" he yelled. "We have to go faster." He fell backward again. Stupid baby and her stupid wishes. Sure, she could make corn grow and crabs crawl out of the toilet, but when something really mattered, when a life was at stake, she just stuck a piece of kelp up her nose.

Boom kicked the oar as hard as he could. Why couldn't he make it work? Why was this happening? Mertyle would die and it would be his fault. It would be this stupid oar's fault too.

"Watch how a Viking descendant does it," Halvor said, pulling the oar with such gusto that he splashed water on Mr. Jorgenson. "It's in my blood, for sure."

Boom kicked the oar again. "Well, it's not in my blood. I'm not a direct descendant of the stupid Vikings! I'm not a direct descendant of anything!"

"You are your mother's direct descendant." A hand pressed down on his shoulder and Boom turned and looked up into his father's eyes. Not the distracted eyes that had peered out from the attic, or the frightened eyes that had stared out the window, watching the weather. These were the eyes that used to greet him every morning when Mrs. Broom was making breakfast and Mertyle was packing her backpack for school.

"I'm nothing like Mom. I'm not smart. I don't solve mysteries. I can't do anything right," Boom cried out.

Mr. Broom sat next to his son and returned the oar to its lock. "You solved the seaweed mystery. If you hadn't found the spots through the magnifying glass, then we'd still be lost."

"That wasn't my idea. It was Mertyle's."

Mr. Broom seemed determined to cheer Boom up. He pulled off his shoe and sock and held out his foot. The toenails were in need of trimming. Otherwise, the foot looked exactly like Boom's, quite a bit longer and wider than the left one. "Did I ever show you my right foot?"

Like, a million times. "Yes," Boom said. "It's big, like mine."

"When I was your age, I never realized that having a bigger foot could be a gift. I didn't know it could give me a kicking advantage. I just tried to hide it because I thought it was kind of weird."

"It is kind of weird," Boom said.

"But you didn't try to hide it, Boom. That's my point. You used it in the best way possible, and that made your mother very proud." Mr. Broom brushed his long hair from his face. "You see, she had a disadvantage as well."

"She had a big foot too?"

"No, she was born color-blind. She never saw a single speck of color her entire life. But, rather than focusing on what others could see that she couldn't, she bought her magnifying glass and began to focus on the tiny world that most of us overlook. And she became an expert. Like you, she found strength in being different."

Boom never knew that about his mother, but he felt too frustrated to allow himself to be comforted. "My stupid big foot doesn't help us now, does it? I can't kick us all the way to Whale Fin Island." He crossed his arms and scowled until his eyes started to burn.

Mr. Broom began to row. "Your foot might not do us any good, but your heart will." He took Boom's hands and curled them over the oar. Slowly and steadily he helped Boom guide the oar back into the water. Slowly and steadily they pushed and pulled until they matched the rhythm of the others. Boom caught on and the boat moved swiftly through the calm sea. Mr. Broom took his hands off the oar and Boom kept the rhythm going all on his own. "I'm sorry I abandoned you," Mr. Broom whispered. He kissed the top of Boom's seaweedy head and returned to his own oar. Boom felt a rush of confidence as the oar became a graceful extension of his own body.

"You know, Dad," Boom called out. "I'm your direct descendant too."

Halvor and Mr. Jorgenson, who had been eavesdropping the entire time, wiped tears from their eyes. "Good to see," Halvor sniffled. "Good to see a father and son back together."

Mr. Jorgenson blew his nose on his shirt. "I miss my old dad."

"Stop your blubbering and row. Row, lads!" Captain Igor yelled. "Row like the devil's breathing at your back."

And they did.

Chapter Thirty:

THOR'S WIND

By midday there was still no land in sight and the air remained as limp as Mertyle's fuzz. Boom didn't think he could row much longer. Halvor passed around some bread and marmalade, but it didn't help much. Boom's arms ached so badly it felt as if his muscles had turned to pulp. Sweat ran down his back and blisters seared his palms.

The others looked equally tired. No matter how much they wanted to press forward, progress slowed as their energy dwindled. Despair found its way under Boom's skin. No land, no merfolk, no sound but the thudding of his heart.

"Row," Captain Igor murmured, resting his head on his oar. The boat almost came to a standstill as the men groaned with exhaustion.

"We've got to keep going," Mr. Broom whispered, stumbling forward to check on Mertyle. But how could they?

"We need wind," Halvor said, letting his oar fall upon the deck. "By the blood of Thor, we need wind. We must call upon Thor."

Boom's oar slipped from his grasp. What good would it do to call upon a dead Viking god? He raised his head and watched as Halvor stomped his way to the ship's bow. The old man struggled onto a crate and held his arms to the quiet sky. "If we all wish hard enough and loud enough, Thor might answer our plea, for sure." He then cleared his throat and bellowed, "All Mighty Thor, God of Direct Viking Descendants, show us your mercy and send us wind."

Mr. Jorgenson stood and raised his arms. "Help us, Mighty Thor."

Boom didn't care who answered their plea — be it a Viking god, the god of Winger's church, or a green menace from the sea. Was it too much to ask for the universe to look kindly upon him just one time? One stinking time?

"I wish we had wind!" he yelled to the sky.

"Yah, that's the spirit," Halvor said. "Louder, so Thor can hear us."

"I wish we had wind," Mr. Jorgenson repeated.

"I wish we had wind," Halvor groaned, shaking both fists.

"I wish we had wind," Captain Igor said as the ship drifted to a complete stop.

Only Mr. Broom had not spoken. All eyes turned to him. Boom waited and wondered and made a silent prayer to Thor that his father would not fall back to his old ways. Mr. Broom cleared his throat. "I wish we had wind," he whispered. The baby looked up. Mr. Broom cleared his throat again. "I really wish we had wind," he said, louder. He stood and shook his fists as well. "Lots and lots of wind!"

"I'll be," Halvor uttered in wonder.

And everyone began to chant — wind, wind, WIND!

But no wind came.

"Jorgenson," Halvor called. "We must chant the Sons of the Vikings oath, so that Thor knows we are direct descendants." And the two men chanted, "If thy brother is hungry, fish for him. If thy brother is cold, build shelter for him. If thy brother is sick, tend to him. If thy brother is lost, help him find his way. Never steal from thy brother."

Boom gasped. *Never steal from thy brother.* He stumbled forward, fumbling in his coat pocket for something forgotten. "Halvor," he said, pulling out the three dollars. "These belong to you."

Halvor frowned. "To me?"

"Yes," Boom said. "It's your change, from the ten-dollar bill." He reached up to Halvor, who still stood on top of the crate. Boom stretched his arm as far as he could. The bills rustled slightly in his hand. Then, just before Halvor took them, they blew out of Boom's grasp.

The wind had arrived.

It flew through Boom's hair and tousled Mertyle's fur coat. She managed to smile, like a crack forming in a snowball. The baby clapped her hands. The men "whoopeed," especially Mr. Broom, who almost lost his balance when an extra-strong gust whipped between his legs. The sea turned choppy and whitecaps formed at each wave's crest, like frosting on cream-filled cupcakes.

"Raise the sail, lads," Captain Igor ordered. Halvor and Mr. Jorgenson pulled the halyard, hoisting the sail until it opened to a full-bodied billow. It was glorious. Boom felt the despair rush from his body. He felt exhilarated. He didn't know if credit should go to Thor, the merbaby, or a freak cold front. It didn't matter. The wind had come.

From the steering oar the captain's voice rose in song:

Hey, hey, away, away.
In the salty air we spend the day.
'Cross blue-green water and ocean spray
Set sail, my lads, set sail.

Set sail, set sail,
Chart your course by a mermaid's scale.
We'll make the journey without fail,
To Whale Fin Island we go.

Hoist the canvas proud and high
Till it touches the endless sky,

> *'Cross the water our ship will fly*
> *Set sail, my lads, set sail.*

The baby seemed to enjoy the singing. She rocked her body as everyone but Mertyle joined Captain Igor in the chorus.

> *Set sail, set sail,*
> *Chart your course by a mermaid's scale.*
> *We'll make the journey without fail,*
> *To Whale Fin Island we go.*

A gull landed on deck. Even though Boom was not a man of the sea, he knew what a gull's presence meant. Captain Igor took out his pocket telescope and searched the horizon. "There she be," he hollered, pointing off the bow. "Whale Fin Island."

Mr. Broom sat beside Mertyle, wrapping his arms around her. The baby voiced her displeasure with a snort and flopped over to the rail. She looked up at Boom and whimpered. He picked her up and she wrapped her slimy arms around his neck. They watched as the tip of the island appeared. Gulls called from overhead, circling as the ship neared.

"Mertyle," Boom called out. "Mertyle, we're here. It's just like in the drawing. Mertyle?" Still holding the baby, he leaned over his little sister. The baby reached forward and pushed the white fuzz from Mertyle's eyes. "Mertyle?"

But this time, his little sister's eyes did not open.

Chapter Thirty-one:

WHALE FIN ISLAND

As soon as the ship came within a stone's throw of Whale Fin Island, the wind died to a breeze. The island looked much smaller than Fairweather. Boom guessed it would take less than an hour to walk its perimeter. It had no trees, just a rocky hill in the middle shaped like a whale fin and dotted with nests. A cacophony of screaming filled the air as the gulls sang out warning cries that strangers had arrived. Dozens of well-fed sea lions occupied the only sandy beach, their tar-colored bodies soaking up the weak winter sun.

Since Vikings design their ships to be beached, that's exactly what Captain Igor did. The sea lions barked their displeasure and scattered as the boat slid onto the sand. "Those creatures reek," Mr. Jorgenson complained, plugging his nose.

"A nasty stench," Captain Igor agreed. "That be what happens when you eat nothing but fish all day long."

Being primarily fish-eaters, both Halvor and Mr. Jorgenson furrowed their brows. Halvor leaned forward and gave Mr. Jorgenson a sniff. "Yah, you don't smell so good yourself." Halvor stuck his nose down his own shirt and winced. "Yah, I don't smell so good either. Maybe we should cook a lasagna now and then."

"Lasagna would be good," Mr. Jorgenson agreed, still plugging his nose.

Captain Igor cast a rope ladder, and Mr. Broom and Halvor carefully carried Mertyle off the ship and laid her on the beach. She remained in some kind of deep sleep from which no one could wake her. Mr. Broom wrung his hands and paced beside his sick daughter. "Now what do we do?" he asked.

Still on deck, Boom studied the paper from the print shop. He could find nothing on the map that indicated exactly where the merfolk might be. The baby eagerly flapped her tail at the top of the rope ladder. Of course! She probably knew where to find her own kind. She could lead them.

Boom carried the baby down the ladder, and as soon as his feet touched sand, the baby dove onto the beach and flopped to the tide line. "We're here!" Boom announced to the barren landscape. "We've brought back your baby."

He cocked his head, listening for a response. The only reply, aside from the frenzied gulls, was a particularly vocal sea lion that, Boom guessed, was telling the intruders to *get lost*. But Boom was not about to get lost. Mertyle's only chance lived here somewhere. He cupped his hands around his mouth. "We've brought back your baby!" Still no reply.

The baby lay on her stomach at the sea's edge. Boom gave her a gentle push. "Go on," he urged. "Go find them." But she didn't go find them. Rather, she shoved her hand into the sand and pulled out a clam. So he made his voice sound mean like one does when instructing a bad dog. "Go. Go home." The baby looked up at him with her big violet eyes. She swam a bit, then came right back. "Go home," Boom ordered again. Her lower lip began to tremble. She dropped the clam and reached out her arms. He stomped his foot and pointed at her. "GO HOME!"

The merbaby growled and smacked her tail in the shallows. Then she swam just a few yards and darted behind a barnacle-encrusted rock, completely hidden from view except for the tip of her tail. "I know you're still there," Boom called out snippily. The tail disappeared. She was no help at all. He looked toward the horizon for signs of anyone or anything. He glanced at the beach where the exhausted crew hunched over Mertyle. He scanned the water around the ship for signs of movement. The dragon figurehead cast an eerie shadow in the water. He turned back to find the baby peering at him over the top of the rock. He thought for a moment that he might actually miss her, despite her ornery nature and the fact that she made his room smell like mud. But she had to go. He sighed with frustration and went to her. She reached out her arms again and he picked her up.

"We'd better search the island," he told the others.

Captain Igor unfolded his telescope. "Good idea, lad. I'll climb to the top of that hill and see what I can see."

Mr. Broom decided to stay and guard Mertyle, so that a sleepy sea lion wouldn't roll over onto her. Boom carried the baby down the beach while Halvor and Mr. Jorgenson went off in the other direction.

The sea lions barked as the boy and the merbaby passed by. At the end of the beach, Boom stepped up onto a rocky ledge and began to navigate around a series of tide pools, dotted with black urchins and red starfish. He stopped every so often to scan the horizon. "Where are they?" he asked the baby. "How do we find them?" She pulled a lister-mint from Boom's coat pocket and popped it into her mouth, wrapper and all. With her fanglike teeth, she consumed the repulsive candy in two bites. Then she reached for another.

On an ordinary day, Boom would have wondered if the cellophane wrapper would melt from stomach acid or if it would reemerge, unscathed. But this was not an ordinary day and all his thoughts focused on finding the baby's mother. "We're here," he called again. "We've brought back your baby. I didn't mean to take your baby. It was a big mistake. I've brought it back."

Halvor and Mr. Jorgenson appeared around the bend. The

island was much smaller than Boom had realized. "Nothing," Halvor said. "Just a lot of seagull droppings, for sure."

"Did you see any conch shells?" Boom asked. The two men shook their heads. Soon after, Captain Igor made his way back down the hill to report that there was no sign from that vantage either.

Where could the merfolk be? Had all this been a terrible mistake? Boom kicked an empty clamshell. What in the name of Thor was he supposed to do now?

Back on the beach, the baby splashed at the tide line while the others gathered around Mertyle. "Night is coming," Mr. Broom said, draping his coat over his daughter. Halvor went back to the boat and got some more bread and marmalade and the canned salmon, which the baby devoured. Boom didn't feel hungry — his stomach had clenched in a knot.

In the middle of the meal, Mr. Jorgenson said what Boom had been thinking ever since they had set foot on the island. "Maybe they're not here. Maybe we read the map wrong."

Captain Igor shook his head. "There's no doubt in me mind. That drawing be an exact replica of Whale Fin Island. No doubt."

Mr. Broom unrolled the map and glanced over at the hill. "It's quite exact. A very skilled artist rendered this."

"This has to be the right place," Boom said, mostly to make himself feel better. "Why else would the baby have a map drawn on its scales? It's got to be there on purpose — like a dog's identification tag." That sounded right.

That made perfect sense. Hope was renewed. "The drawing is the baby's address, confirmed by the map on the conch shell. This has to be the right place. It just *has* to be."

Everyone nodded and passed around a jug of water.

"If we build a fire, we might get the merfolk's attention," Boom suggested.

"That's a great idea," Mr. Broom said. "Let's collect driftwood."

Boom stood, relieved to be doing something. Anything was better than sitting around, watching helplessly as the curse suffocated Mertyle. If he had been home the morning the twister arrived, he wouldn't have sat around helpless. He would have held on to his mother. He was strong; he could have saved her. Here was his opportunity to save Mertyle, yet it was going all wrong. Building a fire was something. Maybe the right thing.

The baby lay at the water's edge as Boom began to search for driftwood. He picked up a soggy piece, and was wondering if it would burn, when a bird's screech pierced the air. Boom turned to see a massive albatross snatch the baby by her tail. It lifted her from the beach and rose very slowly into the air, the weight almost too much of a burden. No way! Just like a twister, the albatross was trying to carry her into the sky. Boom screamed at the bird. "Stop! Drop that!" It continued to rise slowly on widespread wings. Halvor and Mr. Jorgenson started throwing rocks. Boom threw one as well, but the bird had flown out of reach.

Boom's brain raced. What could he do? The baby opened

her mouth in a silent scream, too terrified to make sound. A few droplets of green blood appeared at the tip of the bird's beak, from which the baby hung. Halvor, Mr. Jorgenson, Mr. Broom, and Captain Igor ran circles beneath the bird, holding out their arms in case the baby fell. The bird began to pump its wings toward the hill. Boom grabbed another rock, but even before he threw it, he knew it would do no good. He screamed again in frustration, kicking at the sand helplessly. Kicking at everything in his path until he came to an empty marmalade jar.

It wasn't over yet. He still had an advantage. He picked up the jar and tossed it gently into the air. As it began its descent, he flexed his kicking foot. He knew that it was going to hurt. Kicking heavy glass wasn't like kicking a red rubber ball. He took a deep breath and kicked the bottom of the jar where the glass was thickest. It didn't shatter. It flew straight through the air and hit the albatross in the belly. The bird screeched, dropping its treasure. Boom ran with outstretched arms as the baby tumbled down. He ran like the wind, leaping over Mertyle, snaking around Mr. Jorgenson, flying past Halvor, and jumping over a snoring sea lion. Just in the nick of time, he caught the falling mer-baby. Green slime sprayed all over his face upon impact, and he fell over backward.

Everyone rushed to see if Boom was okay. "I'm fine," he mumbled as they helped him sit up. The baby seemed fine as well, for she started growling at the men.

"That be a glorious kick," Captain Igor said. "You could go professional, lad."

The albatross circled, calling out what Boom suspected were bird obscenities. Then it flew back to the hill.

"I'm so proud of you, Boom." Mr. Broom smiled but it was fleeting, for his face clouded again with worry. "We'd better make that fire."

"Erik the Red was a magnificent kicker," Halvor boasted as he gathered odd bits of driftwood. "Did I ever tell you the story of how Erik the Red invented Kick the Ball Against the Wall?" Boom shook his head, in no mood for one of Halvor's long stories. Fortunately, Mr. Jorgenson found a large, dry log and asked Halvor to help move it.

Still catching his breath, Boom wiped slime off his face. The baby settled in his lap. "Just to let you know, in case you've lost count, this is the third time I've saved your life." He gave her a long, hard look. "If you want to thank me, then find your mother. We need her to lift the curse." The baby blinked and nodded. She understood. But would she do anything? *Could* she do anything?

On the horizon, a crescent moon rose, casting its glow over a calm sea. The baby rested her head on Boom's shoulder and began to sing her sad song. Boom hated that song because it made him want to cry. He fought back his tears, fought back the fear that they had come all this way for nothing — that the baby's mother could be looking in another corner of the world for her child.

Smoke drifted past as the fire crackled. Mertyle lay against her father's chest, the magnifying glass at her side. Mr. Broom hung his head, and the others wiped tears from their cheeks as the baby's song wound its way among them, fanning the flames with notes of sadness. As the merbaby continued her song, a green tear rolled down her cheek. Though they came from different lands, though their skin was fed by different kinds of blood and their tears were different colors, Boom realized that at that very moment they shared the same feeling — the fear of losing someone you love. It had feelings too. *She* had feelings too.

"There's nothing to worry about," Boom lied, trying to comfort the little creature. He took off his coat and covered the baby's shoulders. Even though she wasn't cold, it just seemed like a nice thing to do. "They will come for you. I know they will." The baby pulled a bit of seaweed from Boom's hair and ate it. "I know you didn't mean to make Mertyle sick." The baby kept looking at him, like she was taking a picture of his face. Like she was trying to memorize it. She touched Boom's nose with a little green finger.

Boom suddenly felt really sleepy. He lay back on the sand and looked up at Polaris, the North Star. His eyelids grew heavy as the blanket of night fell over the beach. "I don't blame you for not granting my wishes," he mumbled. "My wishes were stupid. I don't need new shoes or a Kick the Ball Against the Wall arena. I just wish I had my family back."

The sea lions nudged one another and began to pull their massive bodies toward the sea. They disappeared into the cold water for an evening swim, leaving the voyagers to sit on the beach — waiting and wishing for the unbelievable to happen.

Chapter Thirty-two:

The MERFOLK'S SONG

Boom had never slept in such a way before. There were no images to haunt him, no worries to torment him. Never had sleep felt so deep and undisturbed, like being sucked into a void without light, without sound, without turmoil of any kind. Yet the void felt warm and buoyant, as though he were floating on clouds. When he breathed, his body inflated with the sensation of relief. And when he exhaled, he felt completely peaceful.

Then a single sound came to the void, cool and refreshing, like a long drink of water. And it enveloped him and protected him as he floated in oblivion.

Was this death?

"Boom, wake up." It sounded like Mertyle's voice. "Boom, everyone else is already awake."

He rolled over, reaching for his pillow, but he grabbed a handful of sand instead. Sand? He stretched out his legs, but rather than hitting the end of his bed, they pressed against something that barked and nipped. It sounded like a sea lion. Boom opened his eyes. The sun had risen and he was lying on a beach with Mertyle leaning over him.

Mertyle!

Her long brown hair tickled his face. He could see her eyes and her skin. The fuzz was gone! And she was talking. Mertyle was back, and that could mean only one thing.

Boom scrambled to his feet. The sudden rush of blood made him dizzy and Mertyle grabbed his arm. He looked down at his feet, where a trail of green slime led from his coat to the water's edge. Mertyle smiled. "They came in the night," she explained.

"They?"

"The merfolk. I saw them. Everyone else was asleep." She giggled with excitement. "Oh, Boom, they were fabulous. One of them touched me and I felt better." She held up her arms. "I'm all better." She did appear to be all better, back to her skinny, skin-covered, knobby-kneed self. Not a single tuft of fuzz to be seen.

"You . . . you saw them?"

"Yes." She got real close. "There were three. Two of them sat right by your feet." Boom felt an eerie sensation and shivered.

"It was so dark I couldn't see their faces, but their scales glowed and the air shimmered all around them." She took a deep breath, like she was about to tell the best part. "I'm fairly certain that the third one was the mother, because the baby stayed next to her. I was burning up under all the fuzz, and when the mother touched me I suddenly felt cool. Minty cool."

Boom was overwhelming happy and overwhelmingly disappointed at the same time. "Why didn't you wake me up?" he asked.

"She didn't want me to."

"She spoke to you? I thought they didn't have tongues?"

"She didn't speak but somehow I just knew that I wasn't supposed to say anything. I can't explain it any better than that. I just knew that no one else was supposed to see her." Boom struggled to understand. He tried to put the fact that Mertyle was cured above the fact that he hadn't gotten to meet the baby's family or to say good-bye. But he couldn't help feeling left out. Mertyle smiled. "Boom, don't feel bad. She sang a song just for you, while you were sleeping. Didn't you hear it?"

A song, just for Boom. Yes, he remembered it. He could feel the aftereffects, even as he stood there, soothing every inch of his body like vapor rub. Minty cool.

"And the baby put this in your hair." She reached forward and plucked out a green crystal, the baby's tear. Mertyle suddenly frowned. "The baby followed her mother to the water and swam away. She looked so happy. She's better off with them, don't you think?"

Boom looked around. No baby flopped at the water's edge, no baby growled or spat. The most amazing discovery of the twenty-first century had gone. "Yes, she's better off."

"She's lucky to have her mother back." Mertyle sighed, then wrapped her arms around her brother. "But I'm lucky too. I have you and I have Dad. Thank you, Boom. Thank you for saving me."

Boom wasn't much of a hugger, but he squeezed back because he was so happy to have a fuzz-free sister who wasn't going to die. And he squeezed back because it helped him hide how sad he felt that it . . . that *she* was gone.

"Boom, glad to see you're finally awake," Captain Igor hollered from the deck of the ship. "There be a good wind a-coming. We'd better get a move on. Go and fetch your father." Halvor and Mr. Jorgenson waved from the rail.

"Where's Dad?" Boom asked. Mertyle pointed to the top of Whale Fin Hill, where Mr. Broom stood, staring out at the sea.

"He was the first one to wake up and see me all better," she explained. "He told me he wasn't going to hide anymore. Isn't that great?"

"Yah. Really great." Boom reached down to grab his slime-covered coat, and when he lifted it, a conch shell fell to the sand.

"The mark of the merfolk," Mertyle whispered. She picked up the shell, but neither of them needed the magnifying glass to see the etching on the shell's pink lip. It wasn't a map of Whale Fin Island — it was a map, though. Mertyle smiled. "I think it's a gift. They've left you a gift."

They had indeed.

"I bet this will take us someplace great," Boom said. For where else would a merfolk's map take a person, but someplace beyond one's wildest dreams? He tucked the shell under his arm.

Boom and Mertyle joined their father at the top of Whale Fin Hill. "We should come back here as soon as we can," he told his children. "I'd like to bring my paints and canvas. I've never seen a sea quite like this one. It will be a magnificent painting."

"That's great, Dad," Boom said as the salty wind blew by, fanning Mertyle's and Mr. Broom's long hair.

"Halvor is right. I need to get back to work." Mr. Broom took Mertyle's and Boom's hands. "I need to get back to this family."

They could have said a lot of mushy things at that moment, but that was not the Broom way. Sometimes it is best not to dwell on the past, lingering over mistakes and tragedies. Sometimes it is best to simply move forward, one big foot at a time, with paintbrush and magnifying glass in hand.

I just wish I had my family back. That's the last thing Boom had said to the baby.

Sometimes it's our wildest dreams that come true, and sometimes wishes are granted. A feeling that Boom had long forgotten cascaded from the tip of his head to the tip of his kicking foot — pure, undiluted joy.

The morning sun warmed the Broom family as they made their way down Whale Fin Hill. Mertyle paused to examine some rock fungus while Boom stopped to pick a rock out of his shoe. "Why, Boom, that shoe has a hole," Mr. Broom noted. "We need to get you a new pair of shoes."

"A new pair of shoes?" Boom asked.

"Certainly. That's the first thing we'll buy when I sell my next painting. Do you have any idea what kind of shoes you'd like?"

Boom's face almost split, he grinned so hard. "Oh, I have an idea."

Out on the horizon, four blue-green tails smacked the water and a song filled the air. The song danced its way to the island, wrapped itself around the ship, curled up and down the mast, and caressed every breathing soul. This time, not a touch of sadness could be heard in the song.

Not a single drop.

LOCAL FAMILY ARRESTED
FOR COUNTERFEITING

Police arrested the Mump family of 1 Prosperity Street when boxes of counterfeit twenty-dollar bills were discovered in the Mumps' garage. Police began to investigate when the fake bills appeared at local Fairweather businesses on Monday.

Witnesses say that a van delivered the bills to Prosperity Street early Monday morning and that Mr. Mump claimed they belonged to him.

A SWAT team arrived at the scene when Mr. Mump barricaded himself in the garage and started throwing cream-filled cupcakes at anyone who tried to enter. The entire gang, including Mr. and Mrs. Mump, their son, Hurley, and their daughter, Daisy, were taken to Fairweather police station to be questioned.

Hurley Mump, no stranger to this newspaper, had accused his neighbor of stealing an alleged merbaby. According to his sister, Daisy, it was only a Molly Mermaid Faraway Girl Doll.

"This is all Boom Broom's fault," Hurley Mump screamed as police escorted him to the squad car.

"Boom Broom had nothing to do with this," said Victor Emmanuel Wingingham, a local boy known as "Winger," who, his mother pointed out, has perfect school attendance.

The Brooms could not be reached for comment. A sign on their door read: GONE FISHING.